THE CITY OF THE SEVENTH HEART

Book Seven of

The Seven Cities of Mars

By

B.K. Anderson

Copyright Page

Copyright © 2026 by B.K. Anderson

This is a work of fiction. Names, characters, places, and incidents are either products of the author's imagination or used fictitiously.

ISBN: 9798995914839

Dedication

For those who listened long enough

to hear the quiet hum beneath life.

For those who learned

that belonging is greater than ownership.

And for every heart

still searching for home.

Also by B.K. Anderson

The Bog Series

- She Stirs
- She Seeks
- She Sows

The Seven Bogs of Mars

- The Seven Bogs of Mars
- The Bog of Patience
- The Bog of Silence
- The Bog of Movement
- The Bog of Restraint
- The Bog of Passage

- The Bog of Interconnection

- The Bog of Seven Hearts

The Seven Cities of Mars

- The City of Enduring Light

- The City of Silence

- The City of Flowing Currents

- The City of the Measured Hand

- The City of Passage

- The City of Interconnection

- The City of the Seventh Heart

Epigraph

"It was not machine, nor mind, nor god.

It was the first awareness given form —

the One-of-One."

A Quiet Reflection

Every city begins as an idea.

Every heart begins as a silence.

The Cities of Mars were never built only from stone, light, or memory.

They were built from relationships. From patience. From movement. From restraint. From passage. From interconnection.

And finally… from understanding.

Asa once believed life survived through strength.

Saxifraga once believed survival

depended upon preservation alone.

But together they learned something

greater:

Life continues because it belongs.

The bees taught this lesson first.

No single bee survives alone.

No city awakens by itself.

No heart truly lives separated from the

whole.

The Seventh Heart was never a place

waiting to be found.

It was the moment all living things

remembered they were already

connected.

Perhaps humanity is still learning this.

Perhaps we all are.

— B.K. Anderson

Table of Contents

1. The Returning Hum

2. Beneath the Living Light

3. The Gathering of the Seven

4. The Listener Awakens

5. The Breath Between Cities

6. Echoes Beneath Stone

7. Children of Resonance

8. The Keepers Return

9. The Quiet Bridge

10.   The Heart Remembers

11.   The Garden Below Mars

12.   The First Belonging

13.   The Song of the Bees

14.   The Living Council

15.   The Seventh Awakening

16.   The City Without Fear

17.   The Voice of the One-of-One

18.   The Opened Path

19.   The Resonance Field

20.   The Child of Two Worlds

21.   The Jar of Light

22.   The Final Listening

23.   The Seventh Heart

Opening Note

The Seven Cities were never meant to rule the world above them.

They were created to wait.

To listen.

To remember what life could become when it learned to live with itself instead of against itself.

This is not the story of conquest.

It is the story of return.

STYLE ANCHOR – DO NOT CHANGE

Write in the style of classic Andre Norton:

- Smooth, flowing narrative

- No choppy or fragmented sentences

- Paragraphs fully developed (4–7 sentences)

- Natural pacing, not rushed

- Descriptive but controlled

- No modern slang or abrupt phrasing

- Maintain continuity of tone throughout entire chapter

- Avoid repeating sentence structure

- Maintain immersive, quiet, observational tone

Story rules:

- Events unfold gradually

- No sudden jumps or rushed conclusions

- Each paragraph connects to the next

- Maintain emotional and environmental continuity

ALWAYS matches this tone exactly.

STARTING PROMPT (Use Every Time)

Use Anderson Norton Style Anchor. Maintain consistent tone.

Do not become choppy.

Do not shorten sentences.

Write full, flowing paragraphs.

Continue in same tone throughout.

1. The Returning Hum
2. Beneath the Living Light
3. The Gathering of the Seven
4. The Listener Awakens
5. The Breath Between Cities
6. Echoes Beneath Stone
7. Children of Resonance
8. The Keepers Return
9. The Quiet Bridge
10. The Heart Remembers
11. The Garden Below Mars
12. The First Belonging
13. The Song of the Bees

14. The Living Council
15. The Seventh Awakening
16. The City Without Fear
17. The Voice of the One-of-One
18. The Opened Path
19. The Resonance Field
20. The Child of Two Worlds
21. The Jar of Light
22. The Final Listening
23. The Seventh Heart

I'd say **23 chapters is perfect** for this final book. It feels complete, but not dragged out.

Chapter 1

The Returning Hum

The hum returned first.

Not loudly. Not as a command or warning. It came softly through the deep chambers beneath the Seventh City, moving through ancient stone with a steadiness so gentle that, at first, even the Keepers believed it to be memory alone.

Yet memory did not alter the air.

Memory did not stir sleeping corridors that had remained silent through uncounted generations.

And memory did not cause the resting lights beneath the lower arches to awaken one by one in slow waves of pale gold.

Asa stood beneath the great inner bridge and listened.

Far above him, hidden beyond layers of living stone, Mars continued its endless turning beneath cold stars. But down within the city, another motion had begun — one older than machinery and deeper than design. The hum carried no single tone. It shifted gently, as though many distant voices moved together within it, joining and separating like currents within unseen water.

Beside him, Saxifraga remained still.

The soft illumination along the chamber walls touched the silver patterns beneath her skin, causing them to glimmer faintly in rhythm with the returning sound. She had not spoken since the hum began several hours earlier. Asa understood why. Some moments became smaller when words were placed upon them too quickly.

The city itself was listening.

Far below the bridge, the gardens stretched outward through layered terraces descending into warm mist. Water moved quietly there now, threading through channels that had once stood dry. The first growths planted seasons earlier had spread farther than either of them expected. Mosses covered stone edges. Pale-rooted vines reached upward through the lower supports. Small drifting insects hovered above the shallow pools while the bees traveled patiently among newly opened flowering clusters.

Life no longer felt borrowed here.

That realization settled deeply within Asa as he rested both hands upon the smooth railing before him. In earlier years, every restored chamber had carried the feeling of temporary survival, as though the cities themselves waited to decide whether humanity deserved to remain among them. But now the Seventh City breathed differently. The air carried warmth. Moisture gathered naturally upon the stone. Even the silence between sounds no longer felt empty.

Something had changed.

Behind them, soft footsteps approached across the bridge.

Asa turned as three Keepers emerged from the eastern passage.

They moved with the same measured balance all the ancient guardians possessed, though their forms no longer appeared as cold or distant as they once had. The flowing lines across their outer surfaces now carried faint traces of organic light, as though the awakening city had begun reshaping even them through long exposure to the living resonance spreading beneath the chambers.

The first Keeper stopped several steps away.

"The lower listening wells have opened," it said quietly.

Its voice no longer echoed with the hard metallic edge Asa remembered from the early cities. Time and awakening had altered them all.

Saxifraga lifted her gaze. "Without command?"

"Yes."

The Keeper paused before continuing.

"The resonance field is expanding beyond projected patterns. Additional chambers are responding."

A faint uneasiness moved through Asa then, though not fear exactly. The cities had awakened slowly across many years. Each required patience, balance, and understanding. But this felt different. Faster. As though something beneath all seven cities had finally recognized itself.

"The Listener," Asa said softly.

None of the Keepers answered immediately.

Far below them, the hum deepened.

Not louder.

Closer.

Saxifraga finally stepped toward the railing beside Asa. Together they watched the golden lights continue spreading through distant terraces hidden beneath drifting mist. One after another, ancient pathways illuminated far below, extending deeper into sections of the city no living being had entered for centuries.

The Seventh Heart was waking.

And somewhere beneath the living stone of Mars, something had heard the bees.

Chapter 2

Beneath the Living Light

The lower chambers had not carried light

for centuries.

Asa understood this the moment the

descent began.

The pathways beneath the upper terraces

bore none of the careful restoration marks

visible throughout the inhabited portions

of the city. No repaired stone lined these

corridors. No guiding resonance threads

had been reawakened by the Keepers.

Even the air felt older here, untouched by the slow return of movement that had gradually spread through the Seventh City above.

Yet the light continued downward.

Soft bands of pale gold flowed beneath the walls themselves, moving through hidden channels buried inside the ancient stone. The illumination pulsed gently with the same rhythm as the returning hum, neither mechanical nor entirely natural. It resembled breathing more than power.

Asa walked beside Saxifraga while the three Keepers moved ahead carrying narrow staffs of living crystal whose surfaces glowed faintly against the deepening dark. Behind them the upper city had already disappeared. Only silence followed now, broken occasionally by the distant murmur of water moving somewhere far below.

The hum remained constant.

At times Asa felt it more within his chest than within his ears.

"The city is guiding us," he said quietly.

Saxifraga glanced toward the illuminated walls. "Not only the city."

Her voice carried a thoughtfulness that caused Asa to look at her more carefully.

For several moments she remained silent before continuing█

"When the first cities were formed, the One-of-One created foundations beneath them that extended deeper than architecture alone. The chambers below were never meant merely for protection. They were places of listening."

"The listening wells," Asa said.

She nodded.

"The ancient races believed resonance itself carried memory. Not memory stored in machines or records, but memory alive within matter. Water carried it. Stone carried it. Even silence carried traces of what had once passed through it."

Ahead of them, one of the Keepers slowed near a narrowing archway whose surface had become almost completely hidden beneath pale-rooted growths. Tiny blossoms opened along the vines as the living light passed near them, their petals unfolding slowly within seconds of illumination.

Asa paused beside them.

"They were dormant."

"Yes," Saxifraga answered softly. "Waiting."

The word settled deeply within him.

That had always been the truth beneath the cities. Waiting. Not abandonment. Not death. The ancient worlds beneath

Mars had not vanished because they failed. They had withdrawn because the balance required for their survival disappeared long ago.

Now the balance was returning.

Not through conquest.

Not through technology alone.

But through relationship.

The bees had begun it without understanding what they carried. Their movement between the bogs, the cities, the gardens, and the living chambers had slowly woven resonance back into places that once stood divided. What began as pollination had become something greater. The cities no longer awakened separately. They had begun responding to one another.

The Keepers stopped.

Before them, the corridor opened suddenly into vast darkness.

Asa stepped forward slowly until the chamber revealed itself beneath the growing light.

The space stretched downward farther than he could immediately see. Massive circular terraces descended layer after layer around a central hollow whose depths disappeared beneath drifting silver mist. Stone bridges crossed open air between the terraces, while tall crystalline pillars rose from below like frozen beams of moonlight.

And everywhere the golden illumination moved.

Lines of living resonance awakened across the walls in widening circles, spreading outward beneath ancient symbols carved directly into the stone itself. Asa recognized none of them completely, though fragments resembled markings he had seen within the earlier cities.

But these symbols felt older.

Much older.

"The First Chamber," one of the Keepers said quietly.

Even their voice carried reverence now.

Saxifraga stepped slowly onto the nearest terrace. Asa followed close beside her while the remaining Keepers remained near the entrance behind them. Far below, hidden beneath the silver mist, the hum deepened again until the stone beneath Asa's feet vibrated gently with its rhythm.

Then the mist began to move.

Not drifting.

Rising.

Slow currents spiraled upward through the center of the chamber while the golden lines along the walls brightened in response. One by one, the crystalline pillars awakened from within, filling slowly with flowing light that traveled upward through their cores like living fire.

Asa felt the hairs rise along his arms.

Something below them was becoming aware.

Saxifraga stopped walking.

For the first time since entering the lower chambers, uncertainty appeared within her expression.

"The Listener is not alone," she whispered.

Then, far beneath the terraces, another hum answered the first.

Chapter 3

The Gathering of the Seven

The answering hum did not rise in conflict.

It joined.

The sound emerged from somewhere deep beneath the First Chamber, carrying a lower resonance that folded itself carefully within the original tone until both moved together through the stone like converging currents beneath dark water. The terraces trembled softly beneath Asa's feet. Far above, hidden among the heights of the vast chamber, thin streams of silver dust drifted from ancient arches untouched for ages beyond memory.

No one spoke.

Even the Keepers remained motionless near the entrance bridge as though some older command had awakened within them.

The mist continued rising through the center hollow.

Slowly at first.

Then with growing purpose.

The silver currents spiraled upward around the crystalline pillars while the golden resonance lines along the chamber walls spread farther outward in widening circles. Symbols long buried beneath darkness emerged one after another across the stone terraces — vast geometric patterns interwoven with flowing curves that resembled rivers, roots, wings, and stars joined together within a single design.

Asa stared quietly at the markings nearest him.

"They are not written like the others."

"No," Saxifraga answered.

Her gaze remained fixed upon the awakening chamber below.

"These symbols existed before the Cities separated."

The words settled heavily within the air between them.

Before the Cities separated.

Asa understood immediately what she meant. Through the long restoration of the Seven Cities, he had slowly learned that each city represented more than architecture or culture alone. Every city carried a single living principle forward through time — patience, silence, movement, restraint, passage, interconnection. They had awakened separately because humanity itself still understood life in fragments.

But beneath the fragments, there had once been unity.

The hum carried that realization now.

Not as instruction.

As remembrance.

Far below, light gathered within the mist.

At first Asa believed it only reflection from the awakening crystal pillars. Yet the brightness slowly condensed into distinct forms moving beneath the silver currents. Tall shapes passed silently through the depths below the terraces, their outlines difficult to hold clearly within the shifting light.

The Keepers lowered their heads.

"The First Ones return to witness," one of them said softly.

Asa glanced toward Saxifraga, but even she appeared uncertain now.

"Not fully returned," she answered carefully. "Perhaps only remembered."

The distinction mattered.

The ancient races beneath Mars had never truly vanished. That truth had revealed itself little by little across the years. They had withdrawn into silence, waiting for resonance to return to the worlds they once guarded. Yet no city had fully awakened enough to call them home again.

Until now.

The rising light deepened from gold into pale white.

One of the crystalline pillars nearest the center suddenly brightened until its interior resembled flowing sunlight trapped within glass. Then another awakened beside it. Then another farther below.

Seven pillars.

Each separated equally around the descending terraces.

Each carrying a slightly different tone within the growing resonance.

Asa felt the realization before the words formed.

"The Seven Cities."

Saxifraga nodded slowly.

"They are no longer awakening alone."

The chamber responded immediately afterward.

A pulse moved outward through the stone beneath them so gently that it resembled the breathing of some enormous living thing hidden beneath the world itself. The resonance spread upward through the terraces, through the bridges, through the pillars and symbols and ancient pathways. Asa felt it pass directly through him without pain or resistance.

And suddenly he saw them.

Not with his eyes entirely.

With memory.

For one brief moment the First Chamber no longer stood empty beneath ancient ruin. Living figures moved along the terraces below. Countless lights flowed across bridges crowded with beings from races Asa had never fully imagined before now. Great gardens spread through the lower levels while streams of living water carried silver reflections beneath vast open ceilings alive with suspended constellations.

No fear existed there.

No division.

Only movement.

Only belonging.

The vision faded almost immediately, yet the feeling remained.

Beside him, Saxifraga pressed one hand quietly against the railing as though steadying herself against the same wave of remembrance.

"The cities remember themselves," she whispered.

Then one of the Keepers lifted its head sharply.

For the first time since entering the chamber, urgency entered its voice.

"The resonance is spreading beyond Mars."

Silence followed.

Asa turned slowly toward the Keeper.

"What does that mean?"

But before it could answer, the seven

crystalline pillars awakened fully

together.

And somewhere far beyond the buried

cities beneath Mars, something answered

the call.

Chapter 4

The Listener Awakens

The light did not fade after the pillars awakened.

Instead, the chamber deepened around it.

Asa stood motionless upon the terrace while the seven crystalline towers continued pouring pale radiance upward through the drifting silver mist. The glow no longer resembled simple illumination. It carried texture now, movement within movement, as though countless unseen currents flowed together beneath the

stone of the ancient world. The resonance

passing through the chamber pressed

gently against his thoughts until even the

silence around him seemed alive with

listening.

Far below, the answering hum continued.

Not distant anymore.

Near.

The First Chamber trembled softly

beneath another pulse of resonance.

Across the terraces, the carved symbols

embedded within the stone brightened in flowing succession while narrow streams of light moved between them like living pathways rediscovering themselves after ages of separation. Asa watched the patterns carefully and slowly began to understand what he was seeing.

The chamber was communicating.

Not through language alone.

Through relationship.

Every line answered another. Every curve joined to something farther away. The symbols did not stand separate from one another any more than the cities themselves truly had. The entire chamber functioned as a single living field whose parts only appeared divided when viewed from too small a distance.

Beside him, Saxifraga drew a slow breath.

"The resonance has crossed the threshold," she said quietly.

One of the Keepers turned toward her. "Confirmation aligns with the ancient records."

"The records survived?" Asa asked.

"Fragments," the Keeper answered.

"Most remained dormant until the Seventh Heart awakened."

The words settled uneasily within him.

Awakened.

Not opened.

Not restored.

Awakened.

Far beneath the terraces, the silver mist continued spiraling upward around the seven pillars. Within the currents, Asa again glimpsed movement among the lower levels of the chamber. Tall forms passed silently through the brightness below, never fully solid yet no longer entirely illusion either. Some appeared almost human from a distance while others carried shapes unlike anything he had seen within the earlier cities. Yet none of them inspired fear. The feeling flowing upward from the depths carried only calm recognition.

As though the chamber itself remembered its people.

Then the hum changed.

A new tone emerged beneath the others — softer than the resonance surrounding it yet somehow deeper. Asa felt it immediately within his chest. The sound resembled neither machinery nor voice. It moved with the steady patience of breathing, ancient beyond measure yet utterly gentle.

The Keepers lowered themselves slowly to one knee.

Saxifraga did not kneel, but her expression altered in a way Asa had never fully seen before. Wonder touched it. And beneath the wonder rested something rarer still.

Reverence.

"The Listener," she whispered.

The chamber answered.

Light gathered suddenly within the center hollow far below the terraces. The silver currents folded inward upon themselves while the pale radiance surrounding the seven pillars bent gently toward a single point beneath the drifting mist. Asa stepped forward instinctively, gripping the stone railing as the brightness intensified.

Something was rising.

Not quickly.

Not dramatically.

With immense patience.

The mist parted little by little until a vast circular structure became visible beneath the chamber floor. At first Asa believed it to be another terrace hidden below the others. Then he realized the surface was moving.

Slowly rotating.

Ancient rings of luminous stone turned within one another deep beneath the First Chamber, each marked with flowing symbols that shifted softly as the resonance passed through them. At the center rested a dark hollow filled with stillness so complete that Asa felt the entire chamber listening toward it.

No sound emerged there.

No light.

Only presence.

The hum surrounding the chamber softened immediately afterward, not from weakening but from response. Like bees settling instinctively around a queen they had long searched for without understanding why.

Asa felt the realization move through him.

"The Listener was here the entire time."

"Yes," Saxifraga answered softly.

Her gaze remained fixed upon the great turning rings below.

"The Listener was never sleeping."

The words sent a faint chill through him.

"Then what was it doing?"

No one answered immediately.

Far below, the rotating rings continued aligning themselves with slow mechanical grace while narrow threads of pale light began extending outward from the central hollow toward the seven awakened pillars. Asa watched the connections form one by one until each pillar carried a direct line into the darkness below.

A network.

Not built.

Alive.

Saxifraga finally spoke.

"It was waiting for life to return willingly."

Silence followed her words.

Asa understood then why the cities had
failed long ago.

Not because their builders lacked
knowledge.

Not because their technology weakened.

They had forgotten belonging.

The realization settled deeply within him
while the chamber continued awakening
around them. The bogs, the bees, the
cities, the Keepers, even the long patience
of Mars itself — none of it had truly been
about restoration alone. The world

beneath the planet had waited for

relationship to return before it allowed

itself to awaken fully again.

The bees had carried that lesson first.

Not conquest.

Not ownership.

Connection.

Below them, the dark hollow at the center

of the rotating rings brightened faintly for

the first time.

A single point of silver light appeared within the stillness.

Then another beside it.

Two lights suspended within the darkness.

Watching.

The Keepers lowered their heads further.

"The Listener sees us," one whispered.

Asa could not move.

The silver lights remained fixed upon the terraces above with neither threat nor judgment within them. Their presence carried only immense awareness, vast beyond anything human thought could easily contain. Yet beneath that awareness rested unmistakable gentleness.

The same gentleness he had heard within the hum.

Then the chamber spoke.

Not aloud.

Within resonance.

Welcome home.

Chapter 5

The Breath Between Cities

The chamber remained silent after the words faded.

Not empty silence.

Listening silence.

Asa stood motionless beside Saxifraga while the resonance continued moving through the First Chamber in slow waves of pale light. The two silver points within the hollow below remained steady, neither brightening nor dimming, yet their presence filled the immense space beneath the terraces more completely than sound ever could. Around them, the seven crystalline pillars continued carrying streams of living resonance upward through the drifting mist.

Welcome home.

The words had not entered Asa's ears.

They had settled directly into memory.

Far above, hidden somewhere beyond countless layers of stone and ancient structure, Mars continued its endless turning beneath cold stars. Yet here within the deep chambers below the Seventh City, Asa felt distance itself changing. The world no longer seemed divided into separate places joined only by travel and time. Something beneath the cities had begun drawing all things inward toward a shared center.

The Keepers rose slowly from their kneeling positions.

Even their movements appeared altered now — quieter somehow, less mechanical than before. The pale resonance flowing through the chamber reflected softly across their surfaces while faint lines of organic light continued spreading beneath the ancient designs woven into their forms.

"The field is stabilizing," one of them said softly.

Another turned toward the lower terraces where the rotating rings continued their slow alignment beneath the mist. "No instability detected within the listening core."

Listening core.

Asa repeated the phrase silently while watching the immense rings below. The structure no longer resembled machinery to him. Machines performed functions. This felt closer to breathing — a living process sustained through balance rather than command.

Saxifraga stepped carefully forward until she stood near the edge of the terrace overlooking the central hollow. The drifting silver currents moved gently around her while the glow beneath her skin answered the chamber's rhythm almost naturally now.

"The Cities were never independent systems," she said quietly. "They only appeared separate because the resonance weakened long ago."

Asa glanced toward the seven awakened pillars.

"So all of them are connected here?"

"Yes."

Her gaze remained upon the rotating rings below.

"The Seventh Heart was always the center."

The realization settled deeply within him.

Across the long restoration of the bogs and cities, each awakening had seemed isolated at first. One city learned patience. Another movement. Another restraint. Each carried its own lesson forward carefully through silence and time. But beneath those separate awakenings, something greater had apparently waited beneath them all.

Unity.

Not sameness.

Harmony.

The hum surrounding the chamber softened again as though responding to the thought itself.

Then Asa noticed something changing along the upper walls.

Thin streams of pale light had begun extending outward from the seven pillars into narrow channels hidden within the stone terraces. The currents spread farther every moment, threading upward through pathways vanishing into distant corridors beyond the First Chamber itself.

"The resonance is moving," he said.

One of the Keepers nodded.

"The pathways between the Cities are reopening."

Asa felt a faint tightening within his chest.

"The old transit corridors?"

"Yes."

Another Keeper turned slightly toward him.

"But not only beneath Mars."

Silence followed.

Saxifraga slowly lifted her gaze from the chamber below.

"The external pathways," she said softly.

The Keeper inclined its head once.

"They are responding."

For several moments no one moved.

Asa remembered fragments gathered slowly through earlier awakenings — ancient references buried within forgotten chambers, hints that the Cities once maintained connections extending far beyond the world beneath Mars. Until now those stories had felt more symbolic than real, remnants from an age too distant to fully trust.

But the resonance awakening below them no longer felt symbolic.

The Listener had answered.

And something beyond Mars had answered in return.

Far below, the rotating rings shifted again.

A pulse of silver light moved outward through the chamber floor before racing upward along the seven crystalline pillars simultaneously. The terraces trembled gently beneath Asa's feet as the resonance spread through the ancient structure with growing strength.

Then the walls began to awaken.

Not merely glow.

Open.

Hidden seams appeared within the stone surrounding the upper chamber while vast sections of ancient architecture slowly separated from one another after ages of stillness. Dust drifted downward through the pale light as narrow bridges extended silently outward from previously sealed terraces far across the immense hollow.

Passageways.

Dozens of them.

Perhaps hundreds.

Asa stared upward into the widening maze of newly revealed corridors stretching through the upper darkness of the First Chamber. Some rose toward distant unseen levels. Others curved downward into depths the light had not fully reached. Yet all of them now carried the same flowing resonance moving outward from the listening core below.

The city was breathing again.

Beside him, Saxifraga rested one hand lightly against the railing.

"They are preparing."

"For what?" Asa asked quietly.

Before she could answer, the two silver lights within the hollow below brightened slightly.

Not with warning.

Recognition.

Then, through the resonance itself, the Listener spoke once more.

The Seven must become one.

The words moved outward through the chamber like living wind.

And far away beneath the buried foundations of the other Cities of Mars, ancient systems began awakening in answer.

Chapter 6

Echoes Beneath Stone

The resonance did not stop at the chamber walls.

Asa understood this as the newly awakened corridors continued opening throughout the vast darkness above them. Ancient bridges extended silently outward from hidden terraces while streams of pale light flowed through passageways untouched for longer than memory easily measured. Dust drifted through the glowing air in slow silver currents, disturbed not by violence or collapse, but by movement returning gently to places that had waited in silence for ages.

The city was remembering how to breathe.

Far below, the listening core continued its slow rotation beneath the rising mist. The two silver lights within the hollow remained steady, watching without judgment while resonance moved outward through the chamber in widening waves. Each pulse awakened another distant pathway. Each pathway answered another buried system farther away.

The Seven must become one.

The words still lingered within Asa's thoughts like an echo moving through deep water.

Beside him, Saxifraga watched the newly opened terraces stretching upward into the hidden reaches of the First Chamber. Her expression carried both wonder and caution now, as though even she had not expected the awakening to unfold this quickly once the Seventh Heart responded.

"The pathways are aligning faster than the records described," she said quietly.

One of the Keepers stepped toward the railing overlooking the lower terraces. Pale light reflected across the smooth curves of its ancient form while faint resonance lines continued spreading beneath its outer surface like veins awakening beneath stone.

"The Listener is no longer operating within isolated response patterns," it answered. "The field has entered convergence."

Asa frowned slightly. "Convergence?"

The Keeper turned toward him.

"The Cities are beginning to function as a unified living structure rather than independent systems."

The truth of that already surrounded them.

Asa could feel it now within the hum itself. Earlier awakenings always carried separation — one city stirring while another remained dormant, one lesson emerging while others still waited beneath silence. But the resonance filling the First Chamber no longer moved in fragments. Patience flowed within movement. Restraint answered passage. Interconnection threaded through them all like living roots beneath unseen ground.

The Cities were not separate ideas.

They were portions of a single understanding.

Far above them, another hidden corridor opened with a low grinding resonance that rolled softly through the chamber.

Asa lifted his gaze toward the sound and

saw an enormous archway slowly

separating along ancient seams nearly

concealed beneath stone growth and

crystalline vines. Beyond it stretched

darkness untouched by the chamber light.

Then faint illumination appeared deep

within the passage.

Not from the First Chamber.

From somewhere beyond it.

One of the Keepers lowered its head slightly.

"Another City has answered."

A quiet stillness moved through the terraces afterward.

Asa felt it immediately — not fear, but awareness. Across the years, each awakening beneath Mars had unfolded with uncertainty. The cities possessed their own histories, their own scars left behind by ages of abandonment and silence. Yet now those distances no longer seemed to matter. Something deeper than memory was gathering them together again.

"The City of Passage," Saxifraga said softly.

Asa turned toward her.

"You recognize the resonance?"

"Yes."

Her gaze remained fixed upon the distant corridor.

"The pathways carried different harmonic signatures once. Each City breathed differently."

The explanation settled naturally within him. Of course they had. The Seven Cities had always reflected different aspects of life itself. Even now he could sense subtle variations moving within the growing resonance field surrounding the chamber — some currents calmer, some sharper, some carrying warmth while others resembled still water beneath moonlight.

Distinct.

Yet joined.

Far below, the listening core brightened gently again.

The rotating rings shifted with slow precision while new streams of pale silver light extended outward into channels deeper beneath the terraces. Asa noticed additional symbols awakening along the chamber floor now, their patterns flowing farther outward than before.

Not random symbols.

Maps.

"The Listener is showing pathways," he said quietly.

The Keepers exchanged a brief glance.

"Yes."

Another pulse moved through the chamber immediately afterward. This time the resonance carried images with it — not fully formed visions, but impressions passing through memory faster than thought. Asa glimpsed distant chambers beneath other cities. Vast

corridors lined with silent gardens.
Towers suspended above underground
seas reflecting pale constellations across
black water. Bridges crowded with living
beings moving together beneath flowing
light.

Then the impressions faded.

But one remained.

Children.

Asa drew a slow breath.

He had only glimpsed them for a
moment, yet the feeling stayed with him

afterward. Young figures moving among the ancient terraces while bees drifted calmly through warm illuminated gardens. No fear. No division. Only belonging so natural it required no explanation.

Saxifraga had felt it too.

"The memory grows stronger," she whispered.

"Memory?" Asa asked.

She turned toward him slowly.

"The Listener does not only preserve the past. It preserves possibility."

The words settled deeply within the chamber silence.

Possibility.

Not prophecy.

Not command.

Potential waiting for choice.

Asa rested both hands upon the smooth railing while the resonance continued breathing around them. He understood then why the Cities had remained

dormant for so long. The world beneath

Mars could not be reclaimed through

force because it was never truly

abandoned territory.

It was trust withheld.

And trust could only awaken willingly.

Far across the upper terraces, another

corridor opened.

Then another.

The growing light revealed bridges

extending outward in every direction

now, weaving through the vast chamber like threads reconnecting an ancient living web. Yet among all the awakening pathways, one passage slowly drew Asa's attention more than the others.

A narrow bridge descending downward.

Deeper beneath the listening core itself.

Unlike the other corridors, no pale light flowed there.

Only darkness waited below.

One of the Keepers noticed Asa watching it.

"The lower descent has opened," it said quietly.

Saxifraga's expression changed at once.

For the first time since entering the First Chamber, true uneasiness touched her eyes.

"The chamber beneath the Listener," she whispered.

Asa looked toward her carefully.

"You know what is there?"

For several moments she did not answer.

Then, far below the terraces, the two silver lights within the listening core brightened together.

And the darkness beneath them answered with another hum.

Chapter 7

Children of Resonance

The answering hum rose from beneath the Listener like distant thunder carried through deep water.

Not violent.

Immense.

Asa felt the vibration move upward through the stone beneath his feet before the sound itself fully reached the terraces above. The newly awakened bridges trembled softly while pale currents of resonance shifted across the chamber walls in widening circles. Around the listening core, the rotating rings slowed almost imperceptibly, as though the ancient structure itself had turned its attention toward the darkness below.

No one moved.

Even the Keepers remained utterly still.

The narrow descending bridge beneath the listening core seemed darker now against the surrounding light, its ancient surface vanishing downward into depths the resonance had not yet fully touched.

Unlike the open pathways spreading through the upper terraces, this passage carried no welcoming warmth.

Only waiting.

Saxifraga stepped slowly closer to the railing overlooking the lower descent. The pale illumination flowing through the chamber reflected faintly within her eyes while the silver markings beneath her skin pulsed gently with the rhythm surrounding them.

"That chamber remained sealed even before the Cities separated," she said quietly.

Asa looked toward her. "You knew of it?"

"Only through fragments."

Her voice carried uncertainty again, though deeper now.

"The earliest Keepers spoke of a place beneath the Listener where the resonance was first shaped into living form."

Far below, the hum answered once more.

Closer this time.

The silver mist surrounding the listening core shifted slowly outward as though displaced by rising currents from below. Asa watched the movement carefully while the resonance passing through the chamber altered in subtle ways around them. Until now the hum had carried calm balance within it, a patient awareness woven gently through the awakening systems of the Cities.

But another feeling moved beneath it now.

Sorrow.

Ancient and quiet.

One of the Keepers lowered its head slightly.

"The memory field is expanding."

Asa frowned. "Memory of what?"

The Keeper did not answer immediately.

Instead it turned toward the descending bridge while pale lines of resonance brightened along its outer surface.

"The first division."

Silence settled heavily afterward.

Asa felt the meaning before he fully understood it. Across the long restoration of the Seven Cities, fragments of the past had revealed themselves slowly — enough to understand that the ancient races beneath Mars had withdrawn willingly after balance collapsed among them. Yet no chamber until now had carried the feeling of the loss itself.

This place remembered it.

Far below, another pulse moved upward through the listening core. The silver lights within the hollow brightened softly while streams of pale resonance spread outward through the chamber floor like roots extending through hidden soil.

Then the visions returned.

Not scattered impressions this time.

Lives.

Asa suddenly stood within another age beneath Mars.

The terraces surrounding the First Chamber no longer rested in ruin or silence. Living gardens flowed across every level while warm rivers of reflected light moved through open channels beneath crystalline arches. Countless beings traveled the bridges between the Cities, their forms varied beyond anything humanity had yet imagined fully, yet none appeared divided from the life surrounding them.

Children moved among them.

Small figures crossed the terraces beside drifting insects and flowering growths while the hum of the Cities surrounded everything like breathing shared between

all living things. Some children
resembled the ancient races Saxifraga had
spoken of in fragments across the years.
Others appeared closer to human. Yet
none carried fear within them.

Only belonging.

The vision deepened.

Asa watched groups of children kneeling
beside shallow pools where pale water
shimmered with living resonance beneath
their fingertips. Others stood among great
flowering gardens while bees drifted
calmly around them in slow golden

currents. The insects did not avoid them.

They moved as though guided by the

same unseen rhythm.

"They learned resonance naturally,"

Saxifraga whispered beside him.

Her voice sounded distant within the

memory field.

Asa understood then that she saw it too.

The children beneath the ancient Cities

had not been taught dominion over life.

They had been taught participation within

it.

The realization settled painfully within him because it revealed how far humanity once drifted from such understanding. Even Earth still measured survival through possession, separation, control. Yet the Cities beneath Mars had survived by teaching something entirely different.

Relationship.

The hum surrounding the chamber deepened again.

Suddenly the vision shifted.

The gardens dimmed.

The flowing bridges emptied.

Fear moved through the memory field like shadow crossing water.

Asa felt it before he saw its cause. The resonance surrounding the Cities had begun fracturing. Not violently at first. Small divisions appeared between groups once joined naturally together. The children sensed it earliest. He could feel their confusion spreading through the terraces while the hum surrounding the Cities weakened little by little.

The bees disappeared.

Not dead.

Gone.

The memory struck Asa with unexpected force.

Without the constant movement between gardens, chambers, and living systems, the resonance beneath the Cities slowly lost cohesion. The pathways between places weakened. The shared harmony holding the ancient world together began separating into isolated fragments.

The Cities themselves had not failed first.

Belonging had.

The vision faded abruptly afterward.

Asa staggered slightly against the railing while the First Chamber slowly returned around him. The pale terraces, the drifting mist, the seven pillars — all remained unchanged. Yet the feeling carried back from the memory field lingered heavily within him.

Beside him, Saxifraga closed her eyes briefly.

"The children remembered longer than the adults did," she said softly.

One of the Keepers looked toward her.

"That aligns with surviving records."

Asa drew a slow breath.

"The Cities were built for them."

No one corrected him.

Far below, the darkness beneath the listening core brightened faintly for the first time. Not with pale silver like the Listener above, but with soft golden warmth resembling distant sunrise

moving beneath deep water.

Then figures appeared within the glow.

Small figures.

Watching upward from the depths below

the chamber.

The Keepers lowered themselves slowly

once more.

"The Children of Resonance," one

whispered.

And from somewhere far beyond the

buried Cities beneath Mars, the sound of

bees answered the hum.

Chapter 8

The Keepers Return

The golden light beneath the listening core continued rising slowly through the mist.

Asa stood motionless beside the railing while the small figures below remained half-veiled within the soft radiance. They did not move toward the terraces above. They only watched, their presence carrying the same quiet awareness that filled the chamber itself. Around them, the resonance flowing through the First

Chamber softened into something warmer than before, less like awakening and more like recognition returning after long separation.

The Children of Resonance.

The words lingered heavily within the silence.

Beside Asa, Saxifraga lowered her gaze briefly as though listening inward toward some distant memory the chamber had stirred awake within her. The silver patterns beneath her skin pulsed gently in harmony with the living currents surrounding them.

"They remained," she whispered.

One of the Keepers turned toward her. "Not fully within physical form."

"But not gone," she answered softly.

The Keeper inclined its head once.

Far below, the golden figures continued standing within the lower glow beneath the listening core. Asa sensed no fear from them. No urgency. Only patience so complete that it almost resembled stillness itself. Yet beneath that patience rested unmistakable awareness.

They had been waiting.

The realization moved through him slowly.

Not waiting for technology.

Not waiting for command.

Waiting for the resonance of belonging to return strongly enough that the Cities could breathe again without fracturing themselves apart.

The chamber trembled softly beneath another pulse.

This time the resonance spread farther upward through the newly opened pathways surrounding the terraces. Ancient corridors brightened one after another while streams of pale illumination flowed outward into distant chambers hidden beyond sight. Yet something else moved within the awakening now.

Movement answering movement.

Far above, a low harmonic tone echoed through the First Chamber from one of the newly opened passageways. Another answered from somewhere beyond the eastern terraces. Then another farther below.

The Keepers lifted their heads simultaneously.

Asa felt the change immediately.

"They are coming," one whispered.

The words barely faded before figures emerged along the distant bridges.

At first Asa believed the resonance itself had formed them from light and memory. Then the shapes grew clearer as they crossed the awakening pathways toward the First Chamber. Tall forms moved with measured balance beneath flowing currents of pale illumination while faint lines of organic light glimmered across their surfaces exactly as they had upon the three Keepers beside Asa.

But these were older.

Much older.

Some carried visible fractures across their outer forms where ages of silence had worn against them. Others moved more slowly, as though awakening fully required effort after such immense stillness. Yet none appeared damaged beyond restoration. The resonance flowing through the chamber touched them gently as they approached, and Asa sensed the Cities themselves helping guide their return.

More Keepers emerged from corridor after corridor.

Not dozens.

Hundreds.

They crossed the terraces in complete silence while the hum surrounding the chamber deepened into layered harmony around them. Some descended from upper bridges hidden high within the darkness above. Others rose slowly from lower passageways newly revealed beneath drifting mist. Yet all moved toward the First Chamber's center with quiet purpose.

"The Keepers are returning to the Seventh Heart," Saxifraga said softly.

Asa glanced toward her.

"Were they all dormant?"

"Yes."

Her eyes followed the approaching figures.

"When the Cities separated, many entered silence beside the systems they guarded. Some likely remained motionless for centuries beyond counting."

The truth of that settled heavily within him as he watched them arrive.

The Keepers no longer resembled cold guardians built only for maintenance and preservation. The resonance awakening beneath Mars had altered them too deeply for that now. Light moved organically beneath their surfaces. Their motions carried subtle individuality. Some paused briefly near awakened symbols along the terraces as though remembering forgotten responsibilities before continuing onward.

They were not machines merely executing commands.

They belonged to the Cities as surely as the gardens, the chambers, or the bees themselves.

One of the newly arrived Keepers approached the terrace where Asa and the others stood. Unlike the three beside him, this one carried no staff of living crystal. Instead, a narrow band of pale gold circled the center of its chest where ancient symbols glowed softly within the resonance field.

It stopped several steps away.

Then bowed its head toward the listening core below.

"The convergence proceeds," it said.

Its voice carried a depth unlike the others — older, quieter, touched by memory itself.

The nearby Keepers lowered their heads in response.

Saxifraga stepped slightly forward. "You remember the First Age."

The ancient Keeper remained still for several moments before answering.

"I remember harmony before separation."

The chamber silence deepened around the words.

Asa felt the sorrow beneath them immediately.

Not bitterness.

Loss.

The ancient Keeper slowly lifted its gaze toward the lower glow where the

Children of Resonance remained watching from beneath the listening core.

"We failed them first," it said softly.

Far below, the golden light shifted gently through the mist.

The Children did not disappear.

They listened.

Asa rested both hands against the smooth stone railing while the awakening chamber breathed around him. Across the long years of restoration, he had often believed the Cities were teaching humanity how to survive again. But now the deeper truth began revealing itself.

The Cities were teaching humanity how to belong again.

Another pulse moved upward through the listening core.

Immediately the newly arrived Keepers across the terraces became still once more. Pale lines of resonance brightened beneath their forms while the seven crystalline pillars surrounding the chamber deepened from silver into soft gold.

Then the Listener spoke.

Not only within Asa's thoughts this time.

Through the entire chamber.

The Keepers must remember what they were created to protect.

The words moved outward like living wind across water.

And for the first time since the awakening began, several of the ancient Keepers lowered their heads in grief.

Chapter 9

The Quiet Bridge

The grief passing through the Keepers did not resemble human sorrow.

It carried no outward despair. No collapse. No anger.

Only recognition.

Asa stood among the awakening terraces while silence settled once more across the First Chamber. Around him, hundreds of returning Keepers remained motionless beneath the flowing resonance field, their ancient forms illuminated by currents of pale gold and silver moving gently through the vast chamber. The hum surrounding the Cities continued breathing steadily beneath everything now, yet a quieter feeling moved within it.

Remembrance burdened by understanding.

Far below, the Children of Resonance remained gathered within the golden light beneath the listening core. They had not withdrawn after the Listener spoke. If anything, their stillness deepened, as though they understood the grief moving through the Keepers without fear or judgment.

The Keepers must remember what they were created to protect.

The words lingered throughout the chamber like echoes carried through living stone.

Beside Asa, Saxifraga watched the ancient Keepers carefully while distant bridges continued awakening farther out within the darkness. More figures still emerged from newly opened corridors beyond sight, though their approach remained slow and measured. No urgency guided them.

Only return.

"The Cities preserved their guardians," Asa said quietly.

Saxifraga nodded once.

"But not their purpose entirely."

Her gaze moved toward the nearest ancient Keeper standing before them.

"When harmony collapsed, the Keepers continued protecting structure, systems, and order. Yet over time many forgot why those things existed in the first place."

The ancient Keeper lowered its head slightly.

"Protection became preservation," it answered softly.

"And preservation became isolation."

The truth settled heavily within Asa.

Across Earth's history, humanity repeated the same pattern endlessly. Systems meant to support life slowly transformed into systems demanding obedience instead. Fear hardened around memory until survival itself became more important than living.

The Cities beneath Mars had not escaped that danger.

Even here, among beings capable of shaping resonance itself, separation had still found a way inward.

Far below, the listening core brightened softly again.

The rotating rings continued their slow movement beneath drifting silver mist while streams of pale resonance flowed outward through the chamber like living roots extending through buried soil. Yet this pulse carried something different within it.

Direction.

Asa felt it immediately.

Across the vast terraces, several of the returning Keepers slowly turned toward one another. Not toward the listening core. Toward each other. For several long moments they remained completely still, as though listening to currents too deep for ordinary speech.

Then one stepped forward.

Another answered from a distant bridge.

A third crossed slowly down from an upper terrace hidden among the pale mist.

The movement spread carefully through the chamber afterward until dozens of Keepers began approaching one another across the awakening pathways. Some stopped in small groups beneath glowing symbols along the walls. Others knelt quietly beside dormant crystal structures newly stirring with resonance. Yet none spoke aloud.

"They are reconnecting," Saxifraga whispered.

Asa watched in silence.

The Keepers moved with extraordinary gentleness now, almost cautiously, as though rediscovering something fragile they feared disturbing through haste. He realized then how long many of them must have existed without true communion. They preserved the Cities. Maintained the pathways. Guarded memory itself.

But perhaps they had done so alone.

The hum surrounding the chamber softened again.

Not weaker.

Closer.

Then Asa noticed another movement farther across the terraces.

The Children of Resonance had begun ascending.

Small golden figures emerged gradually from beneath the listening core, crossing the narrow descending bridge hidden within the lower mist. Their forms remained partly woven from light itself, difficult to hold clearly within ordinary sight, yet each carried unmistakable presence now.

The Keepers saw them immediately.

Across the chamber, movement ceased.

No command passed between them. No signal. Yet every Keeper became utterly still while the Children crossed slowly upward toward the terraces above.

Asa felt his breath tighten slightly.

The Children carried no fear at all.

They moved among the ancient Keepers exactly as bees moved among flowering gardens — naturally, without hesitation or suspicion. One small figure paused beside a fractured Keeper standing near the lower bridge. The ancient guardian lowered itself carefully onto one knee while soft golden resonance flowed outward between them.

The fracture across the Keeper's chest brightened faintly.

Then slowly began healing.

No one spoke.

More Children crossed the terraces afterward.

Wherever they passed, damaged surfaces along the Keepers softened beneath flowing resonance. Ancient cracks sealed gradually. Dimmed symbols brightened once more. Yet the changes unfolding were not merely physical.

The chamber itself felt lighter.

As though some burden carried silently for ages had finally begun loosening its hold upon the Cities.

"They remember each other," Saxifraga whispered.

Asa looked toward her.

"The Keepers and the Children?"

"Yes."

Her eyes remained fixed upon the awakening terraces.

"They were never meant to exist separately."

Far above, another hidden bridge extended slowly outward from the darkness with a low harmonic tone rolling gently through the chamber. The growing resonance field spread toward it immediately, weaving pale streams of light along the ancient structure as though welcoming it back into the living network surrounding the Seventh Heart.

The city continued breathing deeper.

The convergence was no longer limited to systems or pathways.

Life itself was reconnecting.

One of the Children stopped suddenly near Asa.

The small figure appeared neither entirely physical nor entirely formed from light.

Soft golden currents moved continuously through its outline while its eyes carried extraordinary stillness for one so young in appearance.

It looked directly at him.

Then slowly lifted one hand toward the bridges stretching outward through the First Chamber.

Asa followed the gesture.

Far beyond the terraces, among newly awakened corridors hidden within the pale mist, a single pathway remained dark.

Not dormant.

Closed.

The Child lowered its hand.

"The Quiet Bridge," Saxifraga whispered.

A faint uneasiness moved through the nearby Keepers.

Asa glanced toward her carefully. "What is it?"

For several moments she did not answer.

Then the ancient Keeper beside them

spoke softly into the chamber silence.

"The bridge where the Cities separated."

Chapter 10

The Heart Remembers

No one moved after the ancient Keeper spoke.

The bridge where the Cities separated.

The words settled through the First Chamber with a weight deeper than sound. Around the terraces, the returning Keepers remained motionless beneath the flowing resonance field while pale currents of light continued threading silently through the awakening pathways.

Yet the chamber itself seemed to grow quieter now, as though even the living systems surrounding them listened toward the distant dark bridge hidden beyond the mist.

Asa followed the Child's gaze once more.

Far across the immense hollow, nearly concealed among drifting silver currents and newly awakened corridors, the dark pathway remained unchanged. No resonance flowed through it. No golden illumination reached its surface. While every other bridge within the chamber breathed with returning life, that one remained untouched.

Not abandoned.

Refused.

Beside him, Saxifraga rested one hand lightly against the railing.

"The Quiet Bridge connected the Seven Cities before the separation," she said softly. "Not physically alone. The resonance moved most strongly through it."

Asa glanced toward her. "What happened there?"

The nearby Keepers lowered their heads again.

For several moments only the hum answered.

Then the ancient Keeper spoke.

"The first fear entered there."

Far below, the listening core pulsed gently beneath the drifting mist. The two silver lights within the hollow brightened faintly while the rotating rings slowed another degree within their endless movement.

Asa felt the chamber preparing memory again.

Not forcing it.

Offering it.

The resonance moved outward softly through the terraces until it touched the dark bridge in the distance. For the first time since Asa noticed it, faint shapes slowly emerged along the ancient pathway.

Figures.

Standing motionless within shadow.

The memory field opened.

Suddenly the First Chamber no longer carried silence or ruin. Living bridges stretched outward beneath flowing light while thousands of beings moved among the terraces in calm harmony. The hum of the Cities surrounded everything like shared breathing beneath a living sky of suspended crystal constellations.

At the center of it all stood the Quiet Bridge.

Unlike the other pathways, this bridge carried no walls or arches around it. It extended openly across the vast chamber, suspended above flowing silver mist with nothing surrounding it except resonance itself. Streams of pale light moved constantly beneath its surface, connecting all seven directions branching outward toward the Cities beyond.

Asa understood immediately why it mattered.

The Quiet Bridge was not merely passage.

It was trust made visible.

Children crossed it freely. Keepers moved calmly between groups gathered along its length. The ancient races stood together there without division while the resonance of the Cities flowed naturally between them all.

Then something changed.

Not suddenly.

Subtly.

A hesitation entered the movement surrounding the bridge. Asa felt it before he fully saw it — a slight tightening within the shared resonance beneath the chamber. Conversations shortened. Movements slowed. Some of the gathered races began withdrawing toward their own pathways instead of remaining within the center flow joining the Cities together.

Fear had no single face.

It entered quietly.

The vision shifted closer.

Asa saw a group gathered near the center of the Quiet Bridge. Several ancient races stood there beside Keepers whose resonance lines pulsed uneasily beneath their surfaces. The hum surrounding the bridge no longer moved smoothly between them. Small fractures had begun appearing within it, barely visible at first yet spreading farther with every moment distrust deepened.

"The resources of the Cities were diminishing," Saxifraga whispered beside him within the memory.

"The balance weakened."

Asa watched the figures carefully.

No war erupted.

No violence began.

Something sadder unfolded instead.

Separation justified itself.

One group withdrew to preserve stability within their own City. Another feared the growing imbalance would spread if the pathways remained fully open. Others argued the resonance should be controlled more carefully until harmony returned.

Protection became caution.

Caution became distance.

Distance became division.

The Quiet Bridge dimmed.

Asa felt the pain of it then — not only within the gathered races, but within the Cities themselves. The living resonance beneath Mars had depended upon movement freely shared between all things. Bees crossing gardens. Water crossing chambers. Knowledge crossing generations. Life crossing boundaries without fear.

Once the movement slowed, the harmony weakened.

The Children sensed it first.

Asa saw them standing near the bridge edges, watching the adults retreat slowly toward separation they did not fully understand. The bees no longer crossed the pathways as freely now. Some gardens darkened. The hum beneath the

Cities fractured into isolated tones
struggling to remain joined.

Then the Quiet Bridge closed.

Not destroyed.

Silenced.

The flowing resonance beneath its surface
faded until the great pathway stood dark
and still between the Cities. One by one,
the ancient races withdrew behind their
own systems of preservation and
protection while the Keepers sealed

pathways to prevent deeper collapse
spreading farther beneath Mars.

The memory shattered gently afterward.

The First Chamber returned around Asa
once more.

Silence followed.

Heavy silence.

Across the terraces, many of the returning
Keepers remained lowered in grief while
the Children of Resonance stood quietly
among them. No judgment moved

through the chamber now. Only understanding.

"The Cities survived," Asa said softly.

"Yes," the ancient Keeper answered.

"But survival alone was never enough."

Far across the chamber, the dark bridge remained waiting within the mist.

The Quiet Bridge.

The place where belonging first fractured beneath fear.

Then the Child standing beside Asa spoke for the first time.

Its voice carried no age at all.

"The heart remembers what the mind tried to protect itself from."

The words moved through the chamber like living resonance.

And deep beneath the listening core, something vast began slowly awakening beneath the stone of Mars.

Chapter 11

The Garden Below Mars

The Quiet Bridge remained dark behind them.

Yet the chamber no longer carried the same weight of grief after the memory faded. Something within the First Chamber had shifted subtly during the witnessing, as though the Cities themselves had finally spoken aloud a truth they had carried silently for ages. The resonance flowing through the terraces still moved with sorrow beneath it, but no longer with concealment.

The heart remembered.

And because it remembered, healing had begun.

Asa stood quietly beside the railing while the Keepers slowly lifted themselves once more from their bowed positions. Across the awakening pathways, pale currents of gold and silver continued threading through the vast chamber like living roots spreading beneath ancient soil. The Children of Resonance moved gently among the terraces now, no longer gathered only near the listening core below. Wherever they passed, dormant systems awakened softly behind them.

Gardens brightened.

Water flowed.

Stone breathed.

The changes unfolding throughout the First Chamber no longer resembled restoration alone. Asa sensed something far deeper returning beneath the surface of things — not merely the repair of damaged systems, but the return of relationship between all parts of the living world beneath Mars.

Far below, the listening core pulsed gently once more.

This time the resonance carried warmth within it.

Not memory.

Invitation.

Several of the Children turned simultaneously toward a newly awakened passage descending along the western terraces. Unlike the darker pathways beneath the listening core, this corridor carried soft golden illumination flowing steadily upward through the stone itself. Warm mist drifted slowly from its entrance while faint currents of living fragrance moved through the chamber air.

Asa noticed the bees first.

A small cluster emerged from the glowing corridor before disappearing upward into the terraces beyond. Moments later another followed.

Then another.

Saxifraga watched them carefully.

"The lower gardens," she whispered.

One of the ancient Keepers inclined its head.

"They have awakened."

The words carried quiet astonishment even within its measured voice.

Asa felt something tighten gently within his chest.

Across all the Cities and bogs restored through the years, gardens had always represented survival first — places where life could begin returning after silence and abandonment. But the resonance surrounding this awakening felt different from survival alone.

Older.

The Children of Resonance began moving toward the illuminated passageway.

Not hurriedly.

Almost joyfully.

Their golden forms drifted softly through the warm mist while the Keepers stepped aside to allow them passage. Asa noticed the reverence within the ancient guardians now. None attempted to lead the Children. None guided them. The Keepers followed instead, as though remembering where life itself once taught them to walk.

Saxifraga turned toward Asa quietly.

"We should go."

Together they crossed the terraces behind the Children while the First Chamber continued breathing around them. The warm illumination deepened steadily as they descended through the western passageway. Unlike the older corridors above, these walls carried flowing growths everywhere now. Pale vines stretched along the stone. Soft flowering mosses glimmered beneath drifting resonance currents. Water moved quietly through shallow channels carved beside the descending path.

Nothing here felt abandoned.

It felt sleeping.

And now something beneath the Seventh Heart had gently called it awake again.

The corridor widened gradually ahead until Asa glimpsed open light beyond the mist.

Then the lower garden revealed itself.

He stopped walking.

The chamber stretching before them surpassed anything he had imagined hidden beneath the Cities of Mars. Vast terraces descended layer after layer into warm golden haze while enormous trees

rose upward through the center levels,
their pale silver branches supporting
drifting clusters of luminous blossoms
overhead. Rivers wound quietly between
the gardens while bridges of living crystal
crossed flowing water alive with reflected
light.

And everywhere bees moved through the
air.

Thousands of them.

Not swarming.

Belonging.

The hum filling the garden differed from the resonance within the First Chamber above. There the sound carried memory, awakening, convergence. But here the tone deepened into something gentler and more intimate.

Contentment.

Asa felt it immediately.

Life flourished here not because it had been commanded to survive, but because nothing within the garden struggled against its place within the whole.

The Children of Resonance moved freely among the terraces below. Some knelt beside shallow pools where pale insects drifted across glowing water. Others rested quietly beneath flowering branches while bees settled calmly upon their hands and shoulders without fear.

Saxifraga stood motionless beside Asa.

For the first time since entering the lower chambers, tears brightened softly within her eyes.

"The first living garden," she whispered.

One of the Keepers lowered its head nearby.

"The origin place."

Asa turned slowly toward it. "Origin of what?"

The ancient Keeper looked across the vast terraces stretching below them.

"The resonance partnership between life and the Cities."

The explanation settled deeply within him as he watched the bees moving through the luminous air. The ancient races beneath Mars had not built their civilization separate from living systems around them.

They had grown within them.

The Cities did not imitate nature.

They participated in it.

Far below, several Children suddenly looked upward together.

Then the garden itself responded.

The great silver trees brightened softly from within while waves of pale golden resonance moved outward through their roots beneath the terraces. Water shimmered. Blossoms unfolded. Bees altered their flight patterns all at once until thousands of tiny movements merged into a single flowing current spiraling slowly upward through the chamber.

Asa felt the living harmony move through him like breath itself.

Not domination.

Not control.

Participation.

Beside him, Saxifraga closed her eyes briefly while the resonance surrounded them.

"This," she whispered softly, "is what the Cities were always trying to remember."

Then somewhere deep beneath the roots of the garden, another pulse answered the Listener above.

And for the first time in ages beyond counting, the Garden Below Mars fully awakened.

Chapter 12

The First Belonging

The garden did not awaken through light alone.

It awakened through response.

Asa felt the truth of this while the living terraces below continued brightening beneath the flowing resonance moving outward from the silver-rooted trees. The warm golden haze filling the vast chamber deepened softly around them while bees crossed the open air in great drifting currents, their movement weaving invisible patterns through the garden itself.

Nothing here operated through command.

Every part answered another.

Water answered root.

Root answered blossom.

Blossom answered bee.

And somewhere beneath them all, the resonance of the Cities answered life itself.

The realization settled deeply within Asa as he and Saxifraga slowly descended the crystal bridge leading into the lower terraces. Around them, the Children of Resonance moved calmly among the awakening gardens while the Keepers followed at respectful distance behind. No hierarchy revealed itself here. No separation between guardian and child, between city and living world.

Only participation.

Warm air carried the fragrance of flowering growths unlike anything Asa had encountered within the upper chambers of Mars. Pale silver leaves drifted gently overhead while soft currents of glowing insects moved above the water channels threading through the terraces below. Even the stone beneath his feet no longer felt cold or mechanical.

It carried pulse.

Not metaphorically.

Livingly.

Saxifraga rested one hand briefly against a nearby tree whose bark shimmered faintly beneath the golden resonance.

"The roots are awake again," she whispered.

The tree answered.

Light moved slowly upward through its silver trunk before spreading outward into the flowering branches above them. Thousands of tiny blossoms unfolded almost instantly in response, releasing drifting particles of pale illumination that floated gently through the chamber air like living pollen.

Asa stared quietly upward.

"The garden recognizes you."

Saxifraga lowered her hand slowly.

"No," she answered softly. "It recognizes the return of balance."

The distinction mattered.

Across the years of restoring the Cities, Asa had often believed the ancient systems beneath Mars responded primarily to individuals — to Saxifraga, to the Keepers, even to himself at times.

But standing within the awakened garden now, he finally understood something larger.

The Cities did not awaken because specific beings controlled them.

They awakened when relationship returned strongly enough for life to trust itself again.

Far below, several Children knelt beside a broad pool where glowing water flowed silently between crystalline stones beneath flowering vines. Bees drifted low across the surface while small silver creatures moved beneath the water like reflections given life.

One of the Children looked upward toward Asa.

Then smiled.

The expression carried such openness that Asa felt unexpected emotion rise quietly within his chest. There was no caution within the Child's gaze. No suspicion. No separation between stranger and kin.

Only welcome.

As though belonging had once been the natural condition of life itself.

The Child lifted one small hand toward the water.

Immediately the pool brightened.

Soft currents of resonance spread outward beneath its surface until faint images began moving within the glowing depths. Asa stepped closer beside Saxifraga while the Keepers remained respectfully behind them.

The water showed memory again.

But older.

Much older.

Asa saw the early terraces beneath Mars before the Seven Cities fully existed. Vast living caverns stretched beneath the ancient world where water, stone, gardens, and resonance systems still developed together in careful balance. The first races moved among them quietly while the Keepers — fewer then, simpler in form — assisted the growing harmony surrounding the chambers.

But the most striking thing was the children.

They appeared everywhere within the memory.

Not protected away from the systems shaping the world.

Included within them.

Children carried seeds between terraces. They guided insects gently between flowering growths. They rested beside the roots of silver trees while ancient races worked nearby shaping resonance pathways beneath the living stone.

No separation existed between learning and living.

One of the Keepers standing behind Asa lowered its head slightly.

"The first belonging," it said softly.

Asa turned toward it carefully.

"What does that mean?"

The Keeper's pale resonance lines brightened faintly beneath its ancient surface.

"The Cities learned that life thrives only when nothing important stands outside the circle of care."

Silence followed.

The memory within the water shifted again.

Asa watched the first great garden expanding beneath Mars while bees moved steadily among newly awakened flowering systems. The children followed them constantly, laughing softly while learning the pathways connecting water, growth, resonance, and movement together into one living cycle.

Then he understood.

"The bees taught them."

Saxifraga nodded slowly beside him.

"Yes."

Her voice carried quiet wonder.

"Not through language. Through participation."

The garden around them deepened its hum as though answering the realization itself.

Bees never ruled the garden.

They connected it.

Without demanding ownership.

Without separating themselves from the life they served.

The ancient races beneath Mars had once built their entire civilization around that understanding.

And humanity had almost forgotten it entirely.

Far above, faint resonance pulses still flowed downward from the First Chamber and the Listener beyond. Yet here within the lower garden, the sound transformed into something gentler — not awakening now, but continuity.

The hum of life remembering itself.

One of the Children approached Asa quietly.

The small figure carried a cluster of pale blossoms woven together with silver threads so fine they resembled drifting light more than physical fiber. Without hesitation, the Child placed the woven circle gently into Asa's hands.

Warmth moved through him immediately.

Not physical warmth alone.

Recognition.

The blossoms carried living resonance within them — faint echoes of countless connections moving together through the garden surrounding them. Asa felt water, root, pollen, breath, movement, memory. None separate from the others.

The Child looked up at him calmly.

"This was always meant for sharing," it said softly.

Then it stepped away again among the terraces while bees drifted peacefully through the luminous air above.

Asa stood silently holding the woven blossoms while the garden breathed around him.

And deep beneath the Seventh Heart, the Cities remembered the first truth they had ever learned:

Life survives together or not at all.

Chapter 13

The Song of the Bees

The woven blossoms continued carrying

warmth long after the Child stepped

away.

Asa stood quietly beside the glowing pool

while soft currents of resonance moved

through the silver threads resting within

his hands. Around him, the lower garden

breathed with calm living rhythm —

water flowing beneath crystal bridges,

luminous insects drifting through warm

air, flowering terraces unfolding gently

beneath the golden light filtering through the vast chamber roots above.

Nothing hurried here.

Nothing demanded.

Life moved through the garden with the quiet certainty of belonging fully to itself.

The realization settled deeply within Asa as bees continued passing steadily between blossoms overhead. Their movement no longer appeared random to him now. Each crossing answered another. Each gathering carried something outward that would nourish

life elsewhere. The garden existed

because relationship moved constantly

through it.

The bees were not separate from the

system.

They were the system in motion.

Beside him, Saxifraga watched the

drifting currents thoughtfully while

several Children of Resonance knelt near

the water's edge guiding small silver-

winged insects between flowering

growths. The insects followed their hands naturally, not trained, not commanded.

Invited.

"The hum is changing again," she said softly.

Asa listened carefully.

At first he heard only the familiar layered resonance filling the chamber — the living pulse flowing upward from the garden roots into the Cities above. But slowly another pattern emerged beneath it. Softer. More intricate. Countless tiny vibrations moving together in shifting harmony.

The bees.

Their flight carried tone.

As thousands moved through the terraces simultaneously, subtle variations in their wing patterns merged into living resonance spreading throughout the garden itself. Asa realized then that the hum surrounding the Cities had never originated entirely from the structures beneath Mars.

Life created part of it.

The bees were singing the resonance into motion.

One of the ancient Keepers stepped slowly beside them.

"The first harmonics are returning," it said quietly.

Asa glanced toward it. "The bees create the resonance?"

"Not alone."

The Keeper lowered its gaze toward the garden.

"But they sustain movement between living systems. Without movement, resonance collapses into isolation."

The words echoed painfully against the memories they had witnessed upon the Quiet Bridge. The Cities had not failed through destruction. They failed when movement between lifeforms slowed beneath fear and separation.

The bees had vanished because belonging vanished first.

Far below, the Children of Resonance slowly began gathering among the central terraces surrounding the great silver-rooted trees. One after another they emerged from the garden pathways carrying blossoms, glowing seed clusters, or shallow crystal vessels filled with luminous water. Yet no ceremony announced itself through command or instruction.

The gathering unfolded naturally.

Like breathing shared among many lives.

Saxifraga's expression softened with recognition.

"The Song Gathering," she whispered.

One of the Keepers inclined its head slightly.

"The oldest surviving resonance practice."

Asa watched the Children carefully.

"What does it do?"

The Keeper remained silent for several moments before answering.

"It reminds life that it belongs to more than itself."

The chamber deepened into stillness afterward.

Across the terraces, the bees gradually altered their movement again. Their drifting patterns narrowed toward the center garden while the hum surrounding the chamber softened into layered harmony unlike anything Asa had heard before. The sound no longer resembled simple vibration.

It resembled voices.

Not words.

Presence.

The Children formed a wide circle beneath the great silver trees while warm light flowed slowly through the roots beneath them. Some placed blossoms into the shallow water channels crossing the terraces. Others rested their hands quietly against the glowing trunks while bees settled calmly among their hair, shoulders, and open palms.

Then the song began.

No single voice started it.

The resonance emerged collectively from the garden itself.

Soft harmonic tones moved upward through the trees while the bees answered in shifting currents of vibration flowing through the chamber air. Water joined next, carrying low crystalline tones beneath the bridges. Then the Children themselves added quiet vocal harmonies woven so gently within the resonance that Asa could no longer distinguish where one sound ended and another began.

Everything participated.

Tree.

Water.

Bee.

Child.

Garden.

The song carried no performance within it.

Only relationship made audible.

Asa felt the resonance move through him slowly, deeper than ordinary hearing. The woven blossoms resting in his hands brightened softly while memory and feeling flowed together beneath the living harmony surrounding the terraces.

He saw the ancient Cities again.

Not during their fall this time.

During their fullness.

Children and Keepers crossing open bridges together. Bees drifting through endless gardens beneath warm crystal skies. Ancient races teaching one another without fear of difference. Water carrying resonance between chambers. The Quiet Bridge alive with movement freely shared between all things.

The Cities had once sung together.

Not metaphorically.

Literally.

Their entire civilization operated through harmony sustained by participation rather than control.

Tears brightened quietly within Asa's eyes before he fully realized it.

Not grief.

Recognition.

Humanity once carried fragments of this understanding too. Earth still remembered traces of it buried beneath music, ritual, storytelling, shared meals, planting seasons, lullabies, prayer. Small remnants survived everywhere people gathered not for power, but for belonging.

The Song of the Bees deepened.

Above them, pale streams of resonance suddenly rose upward through the chamber ceiling toward the First Chamber beyond. Asa felt the living harmony spreading outward into the awakening Cities themselves. Far beyond the garden below Mars, ancient systems answered gently in return.

The resonance was no longer rebuilding isolated places.

It was teaching the Cities how to breathe together again.

Beside Asa, Saxifraga slowly closed her eyes while the song surrounded them.

"The Listener hears it," she whispered.

Far above, somewhere beyond stone, mist, and the rotating rings of the listening core, a deep pulse answered softly through the resonance field.

The Children smiled.

The bees altered their flight once more.

And throughout the buried Cities beneath Mars, the ancient hum of belonging began returning to life.

Chapter 14

The Living Council

The First Chamber had grown brighter since the awakening of the Children.

Not because additional lights had appeared, nor because the resonance field had increased in strength. The change came from something less easily measured. Movement flowed differently now. The Keepers no longer stood apart along distant terraces guarding isolated systems. The Children of Resonance moved among them freely, and wherever they traveled, old distances seemed to diminish.

The terraces no longer felt like separate levels within an ancient structure.

They felt like parts of a living whole.

Asa stood beside Saxifraga upon one of the higher bridges overlooking the vast chamber below. The listening core continued its slow rotation beneath drifting silver mist while the great crystalline pillars carried their steady currents of pale light upward through the ancient stone. Yet it was not the machinery that held his attention.

It was the gathering.

Across the terraces, representatives from the awakening Cities had begun arriving.

Some traveled through newly opened pathways carrying the resonance signatures of Passage, Silence, and Movement. Others emerged from chambers that had remained hidden since before the separation. The ancient races did not arrive in military formations nor beneath banners of authority. They came quietly, crossing the bridges in small groups, listening as much as speaking.

No command had summoned them.

The awakening itself had called them.

"The Cities remember what they once were," Saxifraga said softly.

Asa watched a group of visitors pause near one of the lower gardens where bees moved among flowering vines. The newcomers knelt beside the growths rather than hurrying toward the central chamber.

"They do not seem eager to govern anything."

A faint smile touched her expression.

"They never gathered to rule."

Far below, another pulse moved outward from the Listener.

The resonance flowed gently through the terraces before spreading into every bridge and corridor surrounding the chamber. As it passed, Asa noticed something remarkable. Small clusters of beings who had never met before began sharing space naturally. Conversations emerged without translators. Memories were exchanged through resonance. Questions moved freely between races separated by centuries of silence.

The council was already forming.

Not around authority.

Around understanding.

One of the ancient Keepers approached from a nearby bridge. Age marked its surface through faint scars and restored fractures, yet the organic light moving beneath its form glowed steadily.

"The gathering continues," it said.

Asa glanced toward the terraces below.

"How many have arrived?"

"More than records predicted."

The Keeper paused briefly.

"Fewer than once existed. More than we believed remained."

The answer carried both sorrow and hope.

Asa understood why.

The separation had not only divided the Cities. It had scattered generations. Entire cultures had withdrawn into silence while others faded into memory. Yet now, little by little, those forgotten threads were returning.

The living network was rebuilding itself.

Near the center of the chamber, the Children of Resonance gathered around the listening core.

Their golden forms reflected softly within the silver currents rising through the mist. They neither directed the assembly nor occupied positions of importance. Yet every group seemed drawn toward them eventually. Conversations softened near their presence. Old fears eased. Even the Keepers appeared calmer when the Children stood nearby.

"The children are doing what the adults once forgot," Saxifraga whispered.

Asa followed her gaze.

"Belonging?"

"Yes."

The word settled quietly between them.

Not agreement.

Not obedience.

Belonging.

The resonance deepened.

For a moment the chamber seemed to inhale.

Across the terraces, voices gradually faded until only the hum remained. Hundreds of beings turned toward the listening core below. The Keepers stood motionless. The Children lifted their eyes.

Even the bees seemed to pause within the warm air.

Then the Listener spoke.

Not with sound.

With certainty.

The Cities are awake.

The words flowed through every bridge and chamber.

No applause followed.

No celebration.

Only stillness.

Because everyone present understood the deeper truth hidden beneath the message.

The Cities had awakened before.

What mattered now was what they would become together.

And for the first time since the Quiet Bridge had fallen silent long ago, a true Living Council stood gathered beneath Mars.

Chapter 15

The Seventh Awakening

The Living Council remained gathered long after the Listener's words faded.

No one hurried away.

No formal proceedings began.

The awakening unfolding beneath Mars seemed to resist every structure built upon urgency. Conversations drifted naturally through the terraces while groups formed and reformed beside gardens, bridges, and flowing channels of resonance. Knowledge moved freely between races who had once lived separated by centuries of silence. Old histories surfaced. Forgotten memories returned. Yet beneath all of it, Asa sensed something deeper still unfolding.

The Cities themselves were changing.

He noticed it first while crossing one of the upper pathways several days later.

The bridge beneath his feet no longer felt entirely fixed.

Not unstable.

Alive.

The stone carried a faint warmth now. Pale threads of resonance moved beneath the surface like currents flowing beneath shallow water. As he walked, nearby illumination brightened slightly ahead of him and softened behind him. The adjustment happened so naturally that it took several moments before he realized the pathway was responding to movement itself.

The city had anticipated his arrival.

Farther ahead, Saxifraga stood beside a terrace overlooking one of the inner gardens. She watched the flowing light for several moments before turning toward him.

"You felt it."

It was not a question.

Asa nodded.

"The pathways are changing."

"They are learning."

The answer caused him to pause.

Learning.

The word seemed impossible when applied to stone, bridges, and ancient architecture. Yet the more he observed the city around him, the less impossible it appeared. Corridors adjusted their illumination according to activity. Water channels redirected themselves toward newly planted growths. Transit pathways opened before travelers reached them and closed gently afterward.

Nothing appeared programmed.

Everything appeared responsive.

The City of the Seventh Heart no longer behaved like a restored machine.

It behaved like an organism.

The realization deepened throughout the following days.

Gardens expanded without instruction. New flowering species emerged along terraces where pollination activity increased. The bees altered their routes constantly, yet every adjustment seemed to strengthen the city rather than disrupt it. Even the Keepers had begun consulting the resonance field before making decisions, as though the city itself now participated in its own guidance.

One evening Asa stood upon a high observation bridge overlooking the central chamber.

Below him, thousands of lights shimmered across terraces stretching beyond sight. Streams of water reflected silver currents beneath crystalline arches. The Children of Resonance moved freely among the gathered races while the Keepers traveled between districts carrying knowledge rather than commands.

The city breathed.

Not metaphorically.

Actually.

The pulse of resonance moved outward through the terraces in slow rhythmic waves resembling inhalation and exhalation. Energy flowed from gardens toward living chambers. Excess resonance returned through deeper pathways. Movement circulated through

the entire structure like blood moving
through a body.

Nothing remained isolated.

Everything participated.

Beside him, Saxifraga rested her hands
lightly upon the railing.

"The Seventh Heart has crossed another
threshold."

Asa watched the living currents move
beneath the stone.

"What happens now?"

For several moments she remained silent.

When she finally answered, her voice carried both wonder and caution.

"The Cities were never intended to awaken separately forever."

He turned toward her.

"The Listener said the Seven must become one."

"Yes."

Her gaze drifted toward the distant terraces.

"And we are beginning to understand what that means."

Far below, the listening core brightened softly.

The silver lights within the great hollow seemed clearer now than they had during the first awakening. The immense awareness watching through the resonance no longer felt distant. It felt present within every part of the city.

The Listener was not located beneath the Seventh Heart.

The Listener existed throughout it.

Asa felt the truth settle within him.

The cities.

The bogs.

The bees.

The Keepers.

The Children.

The races.

The resonance connecting them all.

None were separate systems.

They were parts of something larger still
learning how to remember itself.

Then a new pulse moved through the
chamber.

Stronger than any before.

The terraces brightened.

The gardens responded.

The crystalline pillars deepened from
silver into gold.

Across the city, every living thing
paused.

For one brief moment, Asa felt seven distant awakenings answering one another across the buried world beneath Mars.

Patience.

Silence.

Movement.

Restraint.

Passage.

Interconnection.

And now the Seventh Heart.

The resonance joined them together.

The awakening was no longer confined to a single city.

The Seven had begun to remember themselves.

And somewhere far beneath the foundations of Mars, something vast stirred in answer.

Chapter 16

The City Without Fear

The change came so gradually that few recognized it at first.

No proclamation announced it.

No Keeper recorded the exact moment.

Yet over the weeks following the Seventh Awakening, an old tension began disappearing from the City.

Asa noticed it while walking through one of the lower garden districts where several races had recently begun sharing living space. Children moved freely between terraces once reserved for separate communities. Gardeners exchanged seeds and growing techniques without concern for ownership. The bees crossed every boundary without hesitation, carrying pollen from one district to another as though the divisions had never existed.

No one stopped them.

No one wished to.

The City of the Seventh Heart was
beginning to live without fear.

Not entirely.

Not yet.

But enough to be noticed.

The ancient races understood what was
happening long before Asa could fully
explain it. Fear had once been woven into
every system beneath Mars. Fear of
scarcity. Fear of loss. Fear of imbalance.
Fear that another group might weaken
what one city struggled to preserve.

Those fears had built walls.

Some visible.

Most invisible.

Now those walls weakened a little more each day.

The resonance field reflected the change.

Where distrust once produced instability, cooperation now strengthened the flow moving through the city. Corridors remained brighter. Gardens flourished more easily. Transit pathways opened naturally between districts that once remained isolated. Even the weather systems forming within the deeper chambers had grown more stable.

Life responded to trust.

The Listener had known this all along.

One evening Asa sat beside a broad channel of flowing water while bees drifted among flowering terraces nearby. The channel had not existed only months earlier. It had formed gradually as the city redirected moisture through regions where new growth appeared strongest.

Across from him, several Children of Resonance sat beside a group of young Keepers.

The sight still amazed him.

The Keepers had once seemed distant and ancient, devoted solely to maintenance and preservation. Now they listened to stories. They answered questions. They walked among the gardens instead of remaining hidden within forgotten systems.

The city had changed them too.

Nothing remained untouched by belonging.

Saxifraga approached quietly and settled beside him.

For a time neither spoke.

The water carried its steady music through the chamber while soft currents of resonance moved beneath the stone.

Finally Asa broke the silence.

"Do you think fear ever completely disappears?"

Saxifraga considered the question carefully.

"No."

He glanced toward her.

She smiled faintly.

"Fear serves a purpose. It warns. It protects. It teaches caution."

"Then what changed?"

Her gaze drifted toward the terraces beyond.

"The city no longer obeys fear."

The answer settled deeply within him.

Fear remained.

But it no longer governed.

The distinction mattered.

Far across the chamber, several races worked together expanding one of the new gardens. Differences remained visible among them. Their histories remained different. Their customs remained different. Yet none of those differences threatened the harmony growing between them.

Unity had not erased identity.

It had given identity room to flourish without conflict.

The lesson spread naturally through the city.

Children learned it fastest.

The Children of Resonance moved easily among every district. Human children followed them. Young members of the ancient races joined them. Games formed. Friendships formed. Shared curiosity crossed boundaries older generations still remembered.

The future was growing before the adults fully understood it.

Later that evening, the Living Council gathered once more beneath the central terraces.

No emergency called them together.

No crisis required action.

They gathered because the city wished to share something.

The realization itself felt unusual.

Yet everyone present understood it.

The resonance field had begun communicating in ways beyond simple messages. It expressed needs. Preferences. Responses. Patterns. The city was becoming increasingly aware of itself.

Not conscious as a person.

Conscious as a living system.

The Listener spoke through the chamber.

The words arrived gently.

Fear preserved life.

Silence followed.

Then another pulse moved through the terraces.

Belonging allows life to grow.

The council listened.

No debate followed.

No disagreement.

Because every being present had already witnessed the truth of those words.

The Cities survived through preservation.

But they awakened through belonging.

The resonance deepened.

Far below, the listening core glowed with warm silver light while the great crystalline pillars answered in gold.

The city breathed.

The gardens breathed.

The gathered races breathed.

For one quiet moment, Asa felt the entire Seventh Heart moving together as a single living organism.

Not many lives sharing space.

One life expressed through many forms.

And somewhere deep beneath the foundations of Mars, the vast presence stirring below seemed to draw one step closer to awakening.

Chapter 17

The Voice of the One-of-One

The silence began three days before the voice arrived.

No warning accompanied it.

No disturbance moved through the Seventh Heart. The gardens continued growing. The Children of Resonance moved freely among the terraces. The bees traveled their endless pathways between flowering districts while the

Keepers carried knowledge and memory throughout the awakening city.

Yet something had changed.

The Listener had become quiet.

Not absent.

Listening.

Asa noticed it first while standing beside one of the upper observation bridges overlooking the central chamber. The immense resonance field continued breathing through the city exactly as before, but the subtle guidance that had accompanied every recent awakening

seemed to have withdrawn deeper

beneath the surface.

The city no longer asked questions.

It waited.

Far below, the listening core glowed

softly within its silver mist while the

seven crystalline pillars surrounding it

shone with steady golden light.

Thousands of beings crossed the terraces

throughout the day, yet an unusual calm

settled over every movement.

Conversations softened naturally.

Footsteps seemed quieter. Even the bees carried themselves with unusual purpose as they moved through the warm currents of air.

Beside him, Saxifraga watched the chamber below.

"You feel it."

Asa nodded.

"The Listener is listening."

A faint smile touched her expression.

"Yes."

He studied her for a moment.

"You knew this would happen."

"I suspected."

Her gaze drifted toward the listening core.

"The ancient records spoke of a stillness that arrives before the final awakening."

The words settled within him.

Final awakening.

For years they had restored the bogs.

For years they had awakened the cities.

Yet beneath all of those journeys something greater had remained waiting.

The One-of-One.

Not hidden.

Patient.

Far below, one of the Children of Resonance paused beside the listening core. Others slowly gathered nearby until a small circle formed around the silver mist. None appeared directed there. They simply arrived.

As though responding to a call too gentle
to be heard.

The Keepers noticed it as well.

Across the terraces ancient guardians
gradually turned toward the center of the
chamber. Hundreds stood motionless
beneath the flowing resonance while
golden currents moved softly beneath
their restored forms.

No command passed between them.

No signal.

Yet every Keeper listened.

The city itself seemed to draw a slow breath.

Then another.

And another.

The rhythm spread outward through every district of the Seventh Heart.

The gardens answered.

The waterways answered.

The crystalline pillars answered.

Even the bees altered their flight patterns, gathering in widening circles above the listening core until a living spiral of gold drifted through the chamber air.

Asa felt the moment approaching.

Not with excitement.

With recognition.

The same feeling accompanied sunrise after a long night.

The same feeling arrived when a seed finally broke open beneath the soil.

Some awakenings could not be rushed.

They arrived only when everything else was ready.

A Keeper approached quietly from a nearby bridge.

Its ancient surface reflected the golden light surrounding the chamber while the resonance flowing beneath its form glowed steadily.

"The lower passage has opened."

Saxifraga's eyes widened slightly.

Asa felt his heartbeat quicken.

"The chamber beneath the Listener?"

The Keeper inclined its head.

"Yes."

Silence followed.

Neither Asa nor Saxifraga spoke immediately.

They had stood upon the edge of many unknown thresholds throughout the years. Yet this one felt different.

Older.

The Children of Resonance had already

begun moving toward the descending

bridge hidden beneath the listening core.

The Keepers followed at a respectful

distance while the bees drifted downward

around them like flowing threads of

living gold.

The city was gathering.

Not for ceremony.

For remembrance.

Together Asa and Saxifraga crossed the terrace and began descending toward the depths below the Listener.

The bridge curved gently through silver mist illuminated by pale currents of resonance. Around them the sounds of the city faded little by little until only the hum remained.

Not many tones.

One.

Unified.

Alive.

The descent seemed longer than Asa expected. The chamber beneath the Listener lay deeper than any place he had yet entered beneath Mars. Ancient stone surrounded them, though the walls no longer felt dormant. Soft patterns of light moved through them like memory returning to long-forgotten pathways.

Finally the bridge opened into a vast circular chamber.

Asa stopped.

The space stretched outward beyond easy sight.

No terraces surrounded it.

No gardens.

No machinery.

Only stillness.

At the center stood a single structure.

It resembled neither throne nor machine nor monument.

A simple circle of luminous stone rested upon the chamber floor while silver resonance flowed through it in slow rhythmic pulses.

The Children gathered quietly around its edge.

The Keepers lowered themselves to one knee.

Even the bees settled.

For several moments nothing happened.

Then the silver light brightened.

Not dramatically.

Gently.

The entire chamber seemed to inhale.

Asa felt the resonance move through him without resistance. Memories surfaced. Journeys returned. The bogs. The cities. The bees. The countless lessons learned through patience, movement, restraint, passage, and interconnection.

All of it flowed together.

Then a presence appeared.

Not before them.

Among them.

Within everything.

The awareness carried neither shape nor boundary. It felt older than the Cities. Older than Mars. Older perhaps than memory itself.

And yet it felt familiar.

As though every living thing already knew it.

The chamber remained utterly silent.

Then the One-of-One spoke.

Not through sound.

Through understanding.

I was never sleeping.

The words flowed through every heart present.

I was waiting.

The resonance deepened.

Asa felt tears rise unexpectedly.

Not from sadness.

Recognition.

The presence continued.

The Cities were never built to preserve life.

They were built to remember it.

The silver currents brightened around the chamber.

The Children listened.

The Keepers listened.

The bees listened.

You restored the gardens.

You restored the pathways.

You restored the Cities.

A pause followed.

Gentle.

Patient.

Then the final words arrived.

But I awakened only when you remembered one another.

The chamber filled with quiet light.

No celebration followed.

No applause.

No proclamation.

Only understanding.

Because every being present knew the truth carried within those words.

The journey had never been about awakening worlds.

It had always been about awakening belonging.

And beneath the living heart of Mars, the first awareness given form finally spoke once more.

Chapter 18

The Opened Path

The chamber remained quiet long after the voice faded.

No one hurried to speak.

No Keeper rose from its kneeling position. The Children of Resonance remained gathered around the circle of living stone while the bees rested among the silver currents drifting through the deep chamber beneath the Listener.

The words of the One-of-One still moved gently through every heart present.

I awakened only when you remembered one another.

Asa stood beside Saxifraga and allowed the understanding to settle within him. Throughout the long years beneath Mars he had searched for answers hidden within ancient systems, forgotten chambers, and buried cities. Yet the truth now felt strangely simple.

The Cities had never been waiting for knowledge.

They had been waiting for relationship.

Far above them, the Seventh Heart continued breathing through its growing resonance field. Asa could feel it now, not as a distant structure but as something connected directly to the chamber surrounding them. The city no longer seemed separate from the One-of-One.

Nothing seemed separate anymore.

The silver light surrounding the circular stone deepened softly.

Then another pulse moved outward.

The response spread through the chamber floor and flowed into the surrounding walls like water entering dry roots. Ancient symbols hidden within the stone awakened one by one. Delicate patterns emerged across the floor in widening circles until the entire chamber glowed with living geometry.

The Keepers slowly lifted their heads.

Not in surprise.

Recognition.

One of the oldest among them rose carefully and stepped closer to the circle.

"The Pathways," it whispered.

The words moved through the chamber like memory.

Asa felt the significance immediately.

Across the years they had reopened passages beneath Mars. Bridges had awakened. Corridors had returned to life. Transit systems once abandoned had begun carrying movement again.

But those had never been the true pathways.

Those had only been reflections.

The real pathways lay deeper.

The One-of-One spoke again.

Not with words.

With vision.

Suddenly the chamber expanded within Asa's awareness.

The Seven Cities appeared beneath him.

Patience.

Silence.

Movement.

Restraint.

Passage.

Interconnection.

The Seventh Heart.

Each shone beneath Mars like living stars

connected through threads of silver

resonance. The threads crossed and

intertwined until the seven awakenings

formed a single luminous network

stretching throughout the buried world.

Yet the vision did not stop there.

The pathways extended beyond the

Cities.

Far beyond.

Asa saw ancient corridors reaching

outward through darkness older than

memory. Vast gates stood dormant within

distant worlds. Resonance moved

between them like currents flowing

through a river system that spanned unimaginable distances.

Not transportation.

Relationship.

The vision deepened.

Some pathways remained bright.

Others had fallen silent.

Many waited.

The same way Mars had waited.

The same way the One-of-One had waited.

Asa understood then why the Listener had spoken of the Seven becoming one.

The awakening beneath Mars had never been intended to remain isolated.

The Cities were part of something larger.

Something ancient.

Something alive.

The vision faded gradually.

The chamber returned.

The silver light continued flowing through the awakened symbols surrounding them while the Keepers exchanged quiet glances across the circle.

Saxifraga stood motionless.

Wonder filled her expression.

"The network survives."

One of the ancient Keepers nodded.

"Fragments."

The answer carried both hope and sorrow.

Many pathways remained broken.

Many worlds had likely fallen silent across the ages.

Yet some still endured.

Enough.

The One-of-One allowed another pulse to move outward through the chamber.

This time the resonance traveled upward.

Far above, the Seventh Heart answered.

Asa felt the response immediately.

Then another answered.

The City of Interconnection.

Then Passage.

Then Restraint.

One after another, the Seven Cities responded through the living network beneath Mars until their voices blended into a single harmony.

The resonance no longer moved from city to city.

It moved through them.

A unified current.

A single living breath.

The Children of Resonance smiled.

Several reached toward the flowing

symbols along the floor as though

greeting old friends.

Nearby, the bees lifted gently into the air.

Their hum deepened.

Warm.

Steady.

Familiar.

The sound moved through the chamber

and joined the greater harmony

surrounding them.

Asa watched them carefully.

For the first time he fully understood what the bees had been doing all along.

Not carrying pollen.

Not carrying resonance.

Carrying connection.

The same lesson repeated through every city, every bog, every awakening.

Life survived through relationship.

The pathways had always existed.

They only required living things willing to cross them.

The silver light brightened once more.

Then the One-of-One offered a final message before the chamber returned to silence.

The path is open.

The words spread gently through the gathered Keepers, the Children, the bees, and the two companions who had traveled so far beneath Mars.

Not a command.

Not a destination.

An invitation.

And somewhere beyond the awakened Cities, beyond the buried world itself, ancient pathways long forgotten began listening once again.

Chapter 19

The Resonance Field

The path had opened.

Yet nothing rushed through it.

No flood of travelers appeared from distant worlds. No forgotten civilizations emerged from ancient gates. The awakening beneath Mars continued in the same manner it always had — patiently, quietly, allowing life to choose its own movement rather than forcing it.

Even so, the change became impossible to ignore.

The resonance field surrounding the Seven Cities continued expanding.

Asa first noticed it several days after the opening of the Path while walking beside one of the upper waterways flowing through the Seventh Heart. The channel wound gently through flowering terraces where children played among the gardens and bees drifted between clusters of pale blossoms. Nothing appeared unusual at first glance.

Yet the city felt larger.

Not physically.

Present.

The awareness moving through the pathways beneath Mars seemed to extend beyond walls, bridges, and chambers now. The resonance no longer remained confined to specific places. It flowed through every living system connected to the Cities.

The gardens felt it.

The water felt it.

Even the air carried traces of it.

Beside him, Saxifraga paused near a flowering arch covered in silver vines.

"The field is stabilizing."

Asa studied the blossoms opening around them.

"The field?"

She nodded.

"The resonance has always existed. But until now it remained fragmented.

Individual cities carried individual currents."

Her gaze lifted toward the distant terraces beyond.

"Now they are becoming one field."

The realization settled naturally within him.

Across the years he had experienced the unique character of each awakening. Patience carried its own tone. Silence possessed another. Movement, Restraint,

Passage, and Interconnection each expressed life differently.

Yet beneath those differences something deeper had always connected them.

Now that connection had become visible.

Far below, the listening core glowed steadily within the heart of the city.

The pulse moving outward from it no longer resembled isolated waves. Instead, a continuous current flowed through every district, every bridge, every garden.

The Seven Cities had begun sharing a common breath.

The resonance field.

Children sensed it first.

They always did.

The Children of Resonance moved effortlessly through the expanding field while human children seemed equally comfortable within it. Asa often watched them gather near the gardens where bees drifted among flowering terraces. They crossed cultural boundaries without hesitation. Ancient races, human settlers, Keepers, and Children shared space naturally.

No instruction guided them.

The field itself encouraged belonging.

One afternoon Asa sat beside a shallow reflecting pool near the central terraces while several children released floating blossoms into the water. The flowers drifted slowly across the surface while bees moved above them in warm golden currents.

A small boy paused beside Asa.

"Can you feel it?"

Asa smiled.

"The resonance?"

The child nodded.

"It feels like everyone is closer."

The answer surprised him because it perfectly described what he had been struggling to understand.

Closer.

Not physically.

Relationally.

The field did not erase differences.

It reduced distance.

The boy returned to the others while Asa remained beside the water.

Nearby, Saxifraga watched the children quietly.

"They learn naturally."

Asa nodded.

"Like the Children of Resonance."

"Perhaps because they have not yet learned separation."

The thought lingered long after the conversation ended.

Far across the city, other changes continued unfolding.

The Keepers reported increasing harmony between districts once separated by centuries of isolation. Knowledge moved freely between races. New gardens emerged throughout previously dormant regions. Water systems synchronized themselves without direct guidance.

The city responded as a living organism.

Not because control had increased.

Because trust had.

One evening the Living Council gathered beneath the central chamber once more.

Representatives from every awakened race sat together among flowing terraces illuminated by silver and gold resonance. The Children of Resonance sat among them. The Keepers stood nearby. Bees drifted lazily through the warm currents overhead.

No crisis had called them together.

The resonance field had.

Asa listened while experiences from every district were shared.

The same pattern appeared repeatedly.

Fear weakened.

Cooperation strengthened.

Differences remained.

Conflict diminished.

No one claimed perfection.

No one expected it.

Yet something undeniable was occurring.

The field encouraged life toward relationship.

Finally one of the ancient Keepers rose.

Its restored form reflected the soft glow surrounding the chamber.

"The field extends beyond the Cities."

Silence followed.

Asa felt his attention sharpen immediately.

Saxifraga looked toward the Keeper.

"How far?"

The Keeper paused.

"Farther each cycle."

The answer carried significance deeper than the words themselves.

The field was growing.

Not through expansion alone.

Through participation.

Every act of belonging strengthened it.

Every bridge crossed willingly expanded it.

Every shared memory, every friendship, every choice to cooperate rather than separate added another thread to the living network.

The resonance field fed upon relationship.

The realization moved through the gathered council.

Far below them, the listening core brightened softly.

Then the One-of-One offered a single thought through the field.

Not a message.

A truth.

Life is strongest where connection flows freely.

The words settled gently across the chamber.

No debate followed.

No explanation proved necessary.

Because every being present had already witnessed the evidence.

The bogs.

The cities.

The bees.

The Children.

The Keepers.

The races.

All had awakened more fully through connection than they ever could have through isolation.

The field deepened.

Warm silver currents moved through the terraces while the city breathed around them.

And somewhere beyond Mars, beyond the ancient pathways now listening once more, the resonance continued spreading quietly into the waiting darkness.

Chapter 20

The Child of Two Worlds

The resonance field continued growing.

Not through force.

Not through expansion alone.

It deepened through relationship.

Across the Seven Cities, pathways once

separated by distance now carried a

shared rhythm. The gardens flourished.

The Keepers remembered. The Children

of Resonance moved freely among the

terraces while the bees traveled their endless routes between blossoms, chambers, and living waterways.

Life no longer gathered around survival.

It gathered around belonging.

Asa often found himself walking the upper terraces of the Seventh Heart during the quieter hours. The city had become large enough that no single mind could fully observe all that unfolded within it. New friendships appeared daily. Ancient races shared knowledge once hidden by centuries of silence. Human settlers and returning peoples worked side by side among growing districts that had stood empty for ages beyond memory.

Yet amid all the changes, one presence continually drew his attention.

A child.

She appeared often near the central gardens where the resonance flowed most strongly. Sometimes she sat beside the waterways watching the bees. Other times she listened quietly to the Children of Resonance as they gathered near the listening core.

No one seemed surprised by her presence.

The city already knew her.

One afternoon Asa found her kneeling beside a pool lined with silver stone. Bees drifted gently above the water while floating blossoms moved through reflected currents of golden light.

The child looked up as he approached.

She smiled.

Not shy.

Not bold.

Comfortable.

As though she had always expected him to arrive.

Asa lowered himself beside the pool.

"The bees seem to like you."

The child glanced toward the insects drifting among the blossoms.

"They like everyone."

The answer made him smile.

"That hasn't always been true."

She considered this.

"Maybe people forgot how to listen."

The simplicity of the words struck him unexpectedly.

Children often reached truths adults spent lifetimes approaching from complicated directions.

The child dipped her fingers into the water.

Gentle ripples spread outward across the pool.

Immediately the resonance within the surface responded. Tiny streams of silver light followed the ripples until the entire

pool shimmered softly beneath the

afternoon glow.

The child watched the movement

carefully.

"It listens too."

Asa followed the expanding circles.

"The water?"

"The city."

The answer carried no uncertainty.

Only observation.

Asa found himself studying her more carefully.

She appeared human.

Mostly.

Yet something within her presence reminded him of the Children of Resonance. The same calm awareness. The same effortless connection to the living systems surrounding the city.

Later that evening he spoke with Saxifraga beside one of the upper bridges overlooking the listening core.

"You've noticed her."

Saxifraga smiled softly.

"Everyone has."

"The child by the gardens?"

"Yes."

Asa rested his hands upon the railing.

"Who is she?"

For several moments Saxifraga remained silent.

Then she answered.

"Perhaps she is the first."

"The first what?"

"The first child who truly belongs to both worlds."

The words lingered between them.

Far below, the listening core glowed steadily while the resonance field moved through the city like shared breathing.

Asa thought of the generations that would come after them.

Children born beneath Mars.

Children raised among humans, Keepers, returning races, and the living Cities themselves.

Children who would never remember the long separation.

Children who would inherit belonging instead of fear.

The realization settled deeply within him.

Everything they had restored pointed toward that future.

Not monuments.

Not systems.

People.

The following morning the Living Council gathered once more.

Representatives from every awakened people sat together beneath flowing terraces illuminated by warm resonance. The Children of Resonance attended as they often did now, while Keepers stood quietly among the outer pathways.

The child arrived as well.

No invitation seemed necessary.

She simply joined the gathering.

No one objected.

The council discussed gardens, pathways, and the continuing expansion of the resonance field beyond the Seven Cities. Reports arrived from distant districts where ancient chambers continued awakening. New communities formed. Old boundaries faded.

Throughout the discussion, the child listened.

Quietly.

Attentively.

When the gathering ended, one of the oldest Keepers approached her.

The chamber grew still.

The ancient guardian lowered itself to one knee.

Not out of authority.

Respect.

The child looked surprised.

"Why are you doing that?"

A soft current of amusement moved through the nearby council.

The Keeper's ancient voice carried warmth.

"Because you represent what we hoped to protect."

Silence followed.

The child glanced around the chamber.

At the humans.

At the returning races.

At the Children of Resonance.

At the bees drifting lazily through the warm air above.

Then she asked the simplest question of all.

"What is that?"

The Keeper's illuminated eyes softened.

"The future."

No one spoke afterward.

Because every being present understood.

The Cities had never existed to preserve the past.

They preserved possibility.

The child stood at the meeting point of countless journeys. Human and ancient. Memory and emergence. Earth and Mars. What had once been separate now lived comfortably together within a single life.

Far below, the listening core brightened.

The One-of-One observed the gathering.

Not interfering.

Witnessing.

A gentle pulse moved through the resonance field.

The city answered.

The gardens answered.

The bees answered.

And for a brief moment Asa saw the future spreading outward through the Seven Cities like sunlight across water.

Not perfect.

Not finished.

Alive.

The child smiled as a bee settled lightly upon her hand.

She watched it carefully before releasing it back into the warm air.

Then she laughed.

A simple sound.

Yet it carried farther through the Seventh Heart than any speech given by councils or Keepers.

Because it was the sound of a world no longer afraid of tomorrow.

And beneath the living light of Mars, the

Child of Two Worlds took her place

among the generations yet to come.

Chapter 21

The Jar of Light

The child's laughter lingered within the
Seventh Heart long after the gathering
ended.

Not because it echoed through the
chamber.

Because it remained within memory.

Asa found himself thinking about it often
during the days that followed. The
resonance field continued growing
throughout the Cities, yet the simple joy

carried by that single moment seemed to reveal something important about the future unfolding beneath Mars.

The Cities no longer awakened for themselves.

They awakened for those who would come after.

Life had begun moving forward again.

One morning Asa walked through the upper gardens where flowering terraces overlooked the central waterways of the Seventh Heart. Bees drifted among the blossoms while warm currents carried the

scent of growing things through the city.

The pathways remained busy with

movement, yet no one seemed hurried.

The city had learned patience.

It had learned trust.

Now it was learning continuity.

Near one of the garden terraces, Asa

found the child once more.

She sat beneath a flowering arch while

several Children of Resonance gathered

nearby. Between them rested a small crystal vessel no larger than both hands.

The vessel glowed softly.

Golden light moved within it like liquid sunlight.

Asa approached slowly.

"What do you have there?"

The child smiled.

"A gift."

One of the Children of Resonance touched the vessel gently.

"The first collection."

Asa knelt beside them.

Within the crystal container he could see tiny streams of golden honey swirling together with faint silver currents of resonance. The substance seemed alive somehow, shifting softly as light moved through it.

"The bees made this?"

The child nodded.

"The gardens helped."

Another Child of Resonance added quietly,

"And the Cities."

Asa studied the vessel carefully.

Across the years he had watched the bees travel between bogs, cities, flowers, waterways, and chambers. Their work had always appeared simple at first glance.

Yet nothing about it had ever been simple.

They carried movement.

Connection.

Belonging.

Now those countless journeys had become something tangible.

A jar of living memory.

Later that day the vessel was brought before the Living Council.

Representatives from every awakened people gathered once more beneath the flowing terraces. The Keepers stood nearby while the Children of Resonance carefully carried the crystal jar into the center of the chamber.

The city seemed unusually quiet.

Almost expectant.

The child stepped forward carrying the vessel with both hands.

The golden light within it brightened softly.

No one spoke immediately.

The jar required no introduction.

Everyone understood what it represented.

Patience from the first bog.

Silence from the listening chambers.

Movement carried by flowing pathways.

Restraint learned through balance.

Passage across opened bridges.

Interconnection woven through all life.

And finally the Seventh Heart itself.

Every lesson lived within it.

Not symbolically.

Literally.

The honey had gathered traces of every awakening.

The child stopped before the council.

"What do we do with it?"

The question moved gently through the chamber.

One of the oldest Keepers lowered its head thoughtfully.

Another representative smiled.

Several Children of Resonance exchanged quiet glances.

Finally Saxifraga stepped forward.

Her eyes reflected the warm light moving within the crystal vessel.

"We give it."

The child blinked.

"To who?"

Saxifraga looked around the chamber.

At the humans.

The Keepers.

The returning races.

The Children of Resonance.

Then upward toward the bees drifting through the warm currents above.

"To everyone."

The answer settled naturally into the silence.

Because the jar had never belonged to a single person.

Or a single race.

Or a single City.

It existed because countless lives had
contributed to it.

The honey represented participation.

A gift created through belonging.

The council agreed.

Not through formal vote.

Through understanding.

That evening a celebration gathered
throughout the Seventh Heart.

Not a grand ceremony.

A shared meal.

People from every district arrived carrying foods, seeds, flowers, stories, and music. The terraces filled with conversation while the resonance field moved gently through the city around them.

At the center stood the crystal jar.

The first jar.

Small portions were shared among those gathered.

Not enough to satisfy hunger.

That was never its purpose.

The gift carried meaning rather than quantity.

Asa accepted a small taste.

The honey seemed warmer than ordinary honey.

Golden.

Bright.

For an instant he felt the movement of countless journeys flowing through memory.

The bogs.

The Cities.

The bees.

The Keepers.

The Children.

The pathways.

All joined within a single sweetness.

Nearby, the child laughed again while several bees drifted around her shoulders.

The sound blended naturally into the celebration.

Asa glanced toward Saxifraga.

She smiled.

"You understand now."

He nodded slowly.

"The jar was never the destination."

"No."

Her gaze moved across the gathering city.

"It was proof."

Proof that life could create something beautiful when it chose connection over separation.

Far below, the listening core glowed softly.

The One-of-One observed in silence.

The resonance field deepened.

The city breathed.

And beneath the living light of Mars, the first jar passed gently from hand to hand, carrying the sweetness of belonging into the future.

Chapter 22

The Final Listening

The gathering ended quietly.

No proclamation marked its conclusion. No signal passed through the terraces commanding those assembled to depart. The living council simply settled into stillness as the resonance field continued breathing gently through the Seventh Heart. Around them, the restored chambers glowed with a warm radiance that no longer seemed to come from the walls, the crystals, or the ancient systems beneath Mars. The light had become part of the life moving through the city itself.

Asa stood beside the upper garden overlooking the central terraces.

The jar rested within his hands.

Soft gold shimmered within the honey gathered from every bog, every city, and every season of patient restoration. The bees had crossed worlds to create it. They had traveled through silence, movement, restraint, passage, and interconnection without ever understanding the names given to those lessons. They had simply lived them.

Below, children moved among flowering pathways while Keepers and returning races shared the same open spaces. No barriers divided them. No guarded corridors stood between one people and another. The city had become what it was always meant to be.

A place of belonging.

Beside him, Saxifraga watched the gardens in silence.

The years rested gently upon them now. Not as burdens. Not as losses. As memory carried forward into living things.

"The city feels different," Asa said quietly.

Saxifraga smiled.

"It remembers itself."

Far below, bees drifted among blossoms growing beside streams that had once run dry. Their steady hum rose through the terraces and joined the deeper resonance of the city until Asa could no longer tell where one ended and the other began.

Perhaps there had never been a difference.

The Listener understood that long before any of them.

Together they crossed the bridge leading toward the First Chamber.

The pathway no longer felt ancient.

Though the stone beneath their feet carried ages beyond counting, life flowed through every surface. Mosses softened the edges of old walls. Flowering vines climbed crystalline supports. Water moved through channels that reflected shifting patterns of light upon the ceilings overhead.

Nothing felt abandoned anymore.

Nothing felt forgotten.

When they entered the First Chamber, the vast space greeted them with quiet familiarity.

The seven pillars continued their slow radiance around the listening core. The

Children of Resonance remained among

the terraces, their forms brighter now than

when they first emerged from memory.

Keepers stood throughout the chamber,

not as guardians watching over silence,

but as participants within a living world.

At the center, the Listener waited.

One by one, seven small figures stepped

forward beneath the living light.

Each carried a different resonance.

The tones spread gently through the chamber, passing through stone, water, gardens, and sky.

Asa felt the frequencies move outward beyond Mars itself.

They were not commands.

They were invitations.

Across distances too great for ordinary travel, ancient races heard the call they had waited generations to hear.

The Cities were ready.

And for the first time since the ancient

separation, the way home had been

opened.

The great rings turned slowly beneath

drifting silver mist.

Patient.

Attentive.

Listening.

Asa approached the railing overlooking the listening core and rested his hands upon the smooth stone.

For a long time he said nothing.

He simply listened.

To the bees.

To the water.

To the children.

To the quiet conversations moving among races once separated by fear.

To the steady breathing of the city itself.

The sounds joined together without effort.

Each distinct.

Each necessary.

Each belonging.

A realization settled gently within him.

The Seventh Heart had never been hidden beneath Mars.

Not truly.

The Seventh Heart existed whenever life remembered its connection to something greater than itself.

The cities had taught that lesson.

The bogs had taught it.

The bees had carried it.

And now the lesson continued beyond them all.

The Listener spoke then.

Not through words.

Not through vision.

Through understanding.

The chamber seemed to widen around him while the resonance flowed softly through every living thing gathered there.

Nothing was demanded.

Nothing was commanded.

Only a single truth remained.

Life endures through relationship.

The understanding moved outward through Asa like warm light.

He glanced toward Saxifraga.

She had heard it too.

No explanation passed between them.

None was needed.

Beyond the terraces, the children laughed softly among the gardens.

The sound carried through the chamber with surprising clarity.

The Keepers listened.

The returning races listened.

Even the city seemed to listen.

And for the first time in countless ages,

the First Chamber held no sorrow.

Only peace.

The listening core brightened gently

beneath the drifting mist.

The silver lights of the Listener watched

the life gathered above.

Not judging.

Not directing.

Witnessing.

Asa looked toward the jar within his hands.

The honey glowed softly in the chamber light.

A simple gift.

A simple beginning.

Yet somehow it contained the story of everything that had brought them here.

Patience.

Movement.

Emergence.

Restraint.

Passage.

Interconnection.

And finally—

Belonging.

The hum deepened gently around the chamber.

The city listened.

The Listener listened.

And within the quiet heart of Mars, life listened to itself once more.

The long waiting had ended.

The remembering had begun.

Chapter 23

The Seventh Heart

Morning came softly beneath Mars.

No sunrise crossed the underground sky of the Seventh City, yet the living light flowing through the chambers brightened gradually as though the city itself understood the rhythm of beginning. Warm gold spread through the gardens. Water reflected gentle patterns across ancient stone. Bees moved from blossom to blossom while the quiet hum of life continued weaving itself through every corridor, bridge, and terrace.

The city was awake.

Not awakening.

Awake.

Asa stood upon the highest bridge overlooking the central gardens and watched the movement below.

Children crossed winding pathways bordered by flowering growths gathered from every restored city. Keepers walked among them without distance or formality. Members of the returning races moved freely through the terraces, sharing knowledge, tending gardens, and helping shape spaces that had remained silent for ages beyond memory.

Nothing appeared hurried.

Nothing needed to be.

The long labor of restoration had given way to something rarer.

Living.

Beside him, Saxifraga rested her hands upon the smooth railing.

The soft glow beneath her skin reflected the city's rhythm so naturally now that Asa could no longer imagine one existing without the other. Across all the years they had traveled together, he had often thought of her as a guardian, a guide, or a bridge between worlds.

Now she seemed something simpler.

Home.

For several moments they watched the gardens in silence.

Then Saxifraga smiled.

"They no longer look upward searching for permission."

Asa followed her gaze.

Children played among the flowering terraces below. They explored. They laughed. They wandered from one group to another without concern for origin, race, or history. The divisions that once shaped entire civilizations carried little meaning to them now.

The future had already begun.

"The Cities taught them something we struggled to learn," Asa said quietly.

Saxifraga nodded.

"They were born into belonging."

The words settled gently between them.

Far below, bees drifted through the gardens in shimmering currents of gold and amber. Their movement appeared almost random at first glance, yet Asa understood differently now. Every bee belonged to something greater than itself.

No single bee carried the future alone. No single bee controlled the hive.

Together they created life.

The realization brought a faint smile to his face.

The bees had known the answer from the beginning.

Humanity had simply required longer to hear it.

A soft resonance moved through the city then.

Not a summons.

Not a warning.

A greeting.

Throughout the terraces, conversations paused briefly. Heads lifted. Children looked toward the center gardens. The Keepers became still.

The Listener had spoken.

Not through words.

Through presence.

The city answered immediately.

The hum flowing through the chambers deepened into quiet harmony while living light brightened beneath pathways, bridges, and distant towers. Across the Seven Cities, the resonance field joined together as one continuous breath moving beneath Mars.

Asa felt it pass through him.

Patience.

Movement.

Emergence.

Restraint.

Passage.

Interconnection.

And now—

The Seventh Heart.

Not a place.

Not a city.

A realization.

The understanding unfolded gently within him.

All the lessons carried by the bogs and cities had always pointed toward this moment. Each awakening restored something necessary. Each lesson healed a different fracture. Yet none of them stood alone.

The Seventh Heart existed when all lessons lived together.

The city understood.

The Listener understood.

And now humanity was beginning to understand.

Far across the gardens, a small child paused beside a flowering terrace and knelt to watch several bees gathering pollen from pale blossoms.

The insects moved calmly around the child.

Unafraid.

The child laughed softly.

The bees continued their work.

A simple moment.

Yet Asa felt unexpected emotion rise within him.

The ancient races once believed the future depended upon preserving knowledge.

Later they believed it depended upon preserving systems.

Then they believed it depended upon preserving themselves.

But the future had never depended upon preservation alone.

It depended upon passing belonging forward.

The child would inherit something greater than memory.

A way of living.

The resonance deepened once more.

The Listener watched.

The city listened.

Life continued.

Asa looked toward the distant terraces where the returning races worked together among gardens that had once existed only in memory. Beyond them stood Keepers who no longer served merely as guardians. Beyond them moved children who would never know the long separation that once divided the Cities.

And farther still, hidden beneath living stone, rested countless possibilities yet to unfold.

The future remained unwritten.

As it should.

Saxifraga slipped her hand into his.

Together they stood quietly above the awakening world.

No great revelation followed.

No final command.

No ending.

Only life continuing.

The bees moved among the flowers.

Water flowed through the gardens.

Children laughed.

Keepers walked beside those they once
protected.

And deep beneath Mars, the Listener
remained patient and awake.

Watching.

Listening.

Remembering.

At the center of all things, the Seventh Heart continued beating—not within stone, nor city, nor race alone, but within the living connection shared by all who belonged.

And in the quiet that followed, somewhere beyond the restored Cities and beyond the gardens of Mars, another ancient silence stirred and listened.

The journey had ended.

And something new had begun.

The ancient guardian nearest the Listener lowered its head.

"The Circle is complete."

Asa looked from the children to the gathered Keepers.

"What are they?"

For a moment only the hum answered.

Then the Listener spoke.

Not aloud.

Not through language.

Through understanding.

The first fixers cared for stone.

These will care for belonging.

The seven children lifted their eyes.

Patience.

Silence.

Movement.

Restraint.

Passage.

Interconnection.

Unity.

The lessons of the Seven Cities no longer lived only within chambers, gardens, and ancient pathways.

They now lived within the next generation.

The Keepers remained bowed.

The bees circled slowly around the children.

The Listener brightened.

And throughout the city, the resonance deepened into a harmony Asa had never heard before.

Not because the Cities had awakened.

Because the Cities had become alive enough to continue without fear.

For several moments no one moved.

No ceremony followed.

No declaration.

The truth required neither.

The Seven Children simply stood together beneath the living light while the city welcomed them as naturally as water welcomes rain.

Beside him, Saxifraga smiled.

"They are the future."

Asa nodded.

"No."

His gaze remained upon the children.

"They are the beginning."

The resonance moved gently through the terraces.

Far beyond the gardens, life continued.

Children laughed.

Keepers walked beside those they once guarded.

The returning races shared stories beneath flowering trees.

Water flowed through channels that had stood dry for ages beyond memory.

And the bees moved patiently among them all.

The future remained unwritten.

As it should.

Saxifraga slipped her hand into his.

Together they stood quietly above the awakening world.

No great revelation followed.

No final command.

No ending.

Only life continuing.

The bees moved among the flowers.

Water flowed through the gardens.

Children laughed.

Keepers walked beside those they once protected.

And deep beneath Mars, the Listener remained patient and awake.

Watching.

Listening.

Remembering.

At the center of all things, the Seventh Heart continued beating—not within stone, nor city, nor race alone, but within the living connection shared by all who belonged.

Below, the Seven Children stood together beneath the living light.

The new Fixers.

The first born of the restored Cities.

And somewhere beyond the pathways of Mars, beyond the silence that had endured since the separation, seven ancient races felt the change and turned their attention homeward once more.

The journey had ended.

And something new had begun.

The End